Rico's gaze was deliberately impertinent

His eyes were fixed on the gap between the edges of Merle's blouse. "I thought I'd made it clear that despite what I may once have imagined I felt for you, I am no longer tempted by anything you have to offer—however charmingly it is displayed."

She was mad to taunt him, but his air of self-righteousness was infuriating.

"From the way you acted a few minutes ago, I could be forgiven for questioning that statement." Her eyes spat fire at him.

"You mean because I kissed you?" Eyebrows arched in disbelief. "But my dear Merle, surely you realized that was merely an experiment to discover how you would react to me after such a long absence? I wanted to know just how fickle you could be."

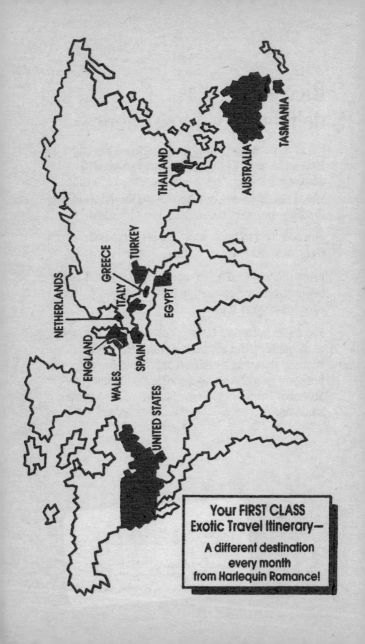

Your FIRST CLASS
Exotic Travel Itinerary—

A different destination
every month
from Harlequin Romance!

SUMMER'S PRIDE
Angela Wells

Harlequin Books

TORONTO • NEW YORK • LONDON
AMSTERDAM • PARIS • SYDNEY • HAMBURG
STOCKHOLM • ATHENS • TOKYO • MILAN

Original hardcover edition published in 1990
by Mills & Boon Limited

ISBN 0-373-03143-2

Harlequin Romance first edition August 1991

O Summer's Pride!
I loved thee from the first,
And, like a martyr,
I was blest and curst.
            'The Lover's Missal'
            Eric Mackay

SUMMER'S PRIDE

CHAPTER ONE

'GRACIAS.'

Merle paid off the taxi, adding a fair tip, and stood watching its tail-lights disappear down the narrow unmade road before inhaling a deep refreshing breath of air tinged with the scent and taste of spring blossoms and the unmistakable tang of the sea.

Waiting while her eyes grew accustomed to the darkness of the Spanish evening, she listened to the soft sounds of the night creatures and the hissing roll of the Atlantic, clearly audible as it licked the expansive stretch of beach a few yards in the distance.

She was back once more on Spain's Costa de la Luz, and it was if the intervening months of sorrow and anxiety had never been. Except this time David wasn't with her.

It was a pity her flight from Gatwick had been delayed. She'd been looking forward to her first real sight of the Villa Paraiso ever since she had signed the contract for its purchase. Fortunately she had no doubts but that she would locate it easily enough even at night! Having studied the ex-owner's photographs of the attractive two-storey villa with its white-painted walls and dramatic wrought-iron railings, its large windows and flower-laden balconies and the attractive garden surrounding it, plus the fact that it had its name boldly printed on a stone plate at its entrance, she could hardly miss it, could she?

Congratulating herself on her forethought in bringing a torch, she searched in her shoulder-bag, producing it with a smile of satisfaction, before stooping to pick up her suitcase and making her way towards the footpath down which the taxi driver had indicated her destination lay.

Not being a total stranger to the area was a great advantage in the circumstances, and she was grateful that this wouldn't be her first sight of the small haven of half a dozen or so holiday homes sprinkled in their luxurious setting, far enough apart to give each occupant complete privacy, yet near enough to allow one to feel one was part of a community.

Walking easily in her flat-heeled shoes, comfortable in her cotton trousers and light edge-to-edge jacket over a long-sleeved blouse, Merle recalled her pleasure at that first sighting of the settlement nearly a year ago, the sense of appreciation linked to an odd sense of *déjà vu*, as if she had known even then that one day she would return to possess a part of it. That was why she hadn't hesitated when, back in England, she'd seen the Villa Paraiso offered for sale in a quality Sunday newspaper, and realised instantly where it was located. At other times she might have been more cautious, but this had to be Fate!

'It's very expensive!' her sister Barbara had temporised, when with a glowing excitement Merle had declared her intentions. 'Are you sure you can afford it?'

'I don't see why not.' Merle had met her worried glance with shining eyes. 'It'll be a marvellous holiday home for you and Grant and Natalie as well as me and Laurie, and when we're not using it we can let it out through an owners' villa service.' She had paused before adding softly, 'Besides, David would have approved. He loved the place. That's why we went back last year.'

'Yes, my love, I know.' Barbara had squeezed her arm in sisterly affection. 'It's just that I don't want you to be disappointed if it doesn't come off. I understand it's not always easy buying property abroad.'

Darling Barbie! Merle thought lovingly of her elder sister as she carefully negotiated the rough path. She owed the other girl so much, and now at last she had found a way in which she could repay just a tiny part of that debt. Fortunately Barbara's reservations had proved unfounded. The villa had been owned by an English couple who, having enjoyed its facilities for a number of years, had decided to join their married children in Canada, and therefore had no further use for it. Negotiations had been straightforward. The key was in Merle's handbag and at some time during the coming week she would go into Seville and collect the deeds from the Spanish solicitor who had acted for the vendor.

How often during the past weeks she had envisaged herself in this situation! Only then, of course, she had imagined the sun would be shining as she took possession of her new domain, not that she would be navigating by the stars! In her mind's eye the location was still quite clear. Turn right by the Villa Rosa... Yes! Merle's torch enabled her to spell out that tiled name on the wall now at her side—this was the silent unilluminated building she had sought... then a hundred yards further along and left... and there it was!

She stopped, as the playful night breeze teased the ebony softness of her hair against her shoulders, placing her suitcase on the ground at her side to enable her to drink in the beauty of her newly acquired Spanish home, a thrill of pure happiness surging through her at the prospect of ownership.

Beneath the starlit sky the white walls of the Villa Paraiso glowed, their smooth surface reflecting every particle of available light. In the darkness Merle's shapely mouth curled into a smile of satisfaction. It was beautiful—just perfect.

Basic furniture had been included in the purchase price, so at least she'd have a bed for the night and some bedclothes to put on it, according to the inventory! Then tomorrow she could start looking around, discover what else she needed to put her own stamp on the villa, arrange for a maid service, find out where the local shops were—all the hundred and one things she had come over by herself to do before sending for Barbara and the others to join her.

A few more steps and she was at the double wrought-iron gates, her fingers on the latch, pressing it down. Nothing happened. Bother the darkness! she thought crossly, juggling with the torch as a cloud momentarily obscured the sickle moon. Her searching fingers found a chain, followed its length and discovered a large padlock, firmly fastened. Ah, well, she sighed, security was good. She supposed she should be pleased about that, although she wished she'd been warned!

Standing back, she surveyed the rough stone walls on either side of the gates, relieved to discover that, although they were about six feet high, with a bit of luck they should be negotiable, though her suitcase would have to wait until she had gained access to the villa and could find some tool or other to break the chain. With a sigh of resignation she found a toe-hold and managed to drag herself towards the top. From there she jumped towards the ground, landing on hands and knees the other side, rubbing one knee ruefully as she rose to her feet. Thank heavens the trousers she was wearing had seen better days. She wouldn't have liked to have ruined a new pair, and her fingers told her these had sustained a ragged tear where they had come off worse in an encounter with a sharp stone. Still, she mustn't complain. In truth she should be grateful that her natural athletic ability hadn't diminished with her twenty-three years and had been sufficient to gain her access to her own property!

Without the suitcase her progress along the garden path was swift, her hand already groping in her shoulder-bag for the purse which contained the key to the Villa Paraiso. 'The Key to Paradise,' she translated in a soft whisper, resolving that she would take steps to improve her tourist Spanish into something worthwhile at the earliest opportunity.

She was still making plans for the immediate future when she inserted the key in the lock of the front door and attempted to turn it. Nothing happened. Damn! This was all she needed—for the lock to have rusted! Visions of having to spend the night sleeping in the garden filled her mind. But hadn't she been assured that the villa was being maintained by a gardener/handyman on a long-term contract? Agitatedly she tried to twist the key once more as her unease increased—again without result. There was only one other possible explanation. She'd been sent the wrong key! Hardly able to believe her bad fortune, Merle stared down at the useless piece of metal in her hand. Perhaps she could get in through a window?

A tour of the outside of the villa proved it impossible. Every window was barred and shuttered. Thoughtfully she stared at the white stone steps leading from ground level to the first-floor balcony, as her heart pounded in sudden anxiety. In the photograph she had they had carried open access from the ground, yet now they were shut off by six-feet-high iron gates with spikes on top—an addition of which she had received no notification and one she certainly hadn't authorised!

A cool breeze shivered across the warm skin of Merle's neck, as for the first time she felt fear stiffen her limbs. The animal sounds she had greeted with pleasure now

seemed to have a hostile echo to them, and was this
dampness she felt in the wind that blew her hair across
her cheek with contemptuous disregard for her comfort?
If she'd been Lucifer himself she could hardly have been
less welcome in paradise, she thought wryly.

Obviously unless she meant to stretch out in the open
she had to find someone to help her. If she could gain
access to a phone she could get a taxi to take her further
up the coast where the tourist hotels lined the beach.
The season here, so far south, was a long one, so even
in early June they would be open, and surely there would
be a bed somewhere for her? Then in the morning she
would locate the estate agent responsible and obtain the
right key.

Now she had found her solution Merle's pulse
quietened. It was unlike her to panic, but the events of
the past year had weakened her, she admitted reluctantly. Only those who fought losing battles would ever
guess how much her spirit had been drained in the long
months of caring and waiting, how much she needed the
peace and solitude this short break had promised her.

Resolutely she pulled herself together, gathering her
energy to make a further assault on the wall. She succeeded, but not without incident. Ruefully she brushed
down her soiled blouse, grimacing at the way it gaped
open across her breasts, two buttons lost forever. As for
her broken fingernails—well, they would grow again.
Somehow she'd got a sharp stone in her shoe though.
That would have to be removed before she took another
step.

As she propped herself up against the wall, her hand
encountered a piece of light card which had been fixed
there and which had previously escaped her notice. For-
getting the pain in her foot, curiously Merle turned her
torch on to the printed words ... *'Prohibido el paso'* ...

Even her limited Spanish could cope with that, as a sense of foreboding filled her. Entry forbidden!

As the small hairs at the back of her neck rose to attention she wondered if it had been meant for her, and if so—why? A qualm of apprehension brought goosepimples to her skin. Here she was in a foreign country, alone at night without transport or means of communication, and entrance to her own property denied! Anger and frustration mixed in equal amounts as she vigorously emptied her shoe of grit.

Vainly she cast her eyes about, hoping to discern a glimmer of light which would suggest habitation. Without some guide she had no way of knowing in which direction to walk to find an occupied villa, neither, she realised miserably, could she guarantee that anyone would understand her request to use their phone or let her over their threshold, especially in the disreputable state she was now in.

It was then that the Villa Jazmin forced itself into the forefront of her mind. Hadn't Rico told her that the Montillas made regular use of it not only for themselves and their friends but also for the workers on their estate? It was just possible that someone would be staying there. Perhaps even Rico de Montilla himself! For a few weeks last year they had struck up a casual fellowship, meeting by chance on the beach, finding an instant rapport... A warm glow of comfort renewed Merle's courage. It might be a long shot, but one worth trying. If Rico was there he would be bound to help her!

Until that moment she hadn't even admitted to herself that part of the attraction of returning to the Costa de la Luz had been the prospect that she might see Rico again and be able to renew their acquaintanceship. How much easier her acceptance into a foreign community would be if she was already known to one of its existing summer visitors! Now the thought of his possible presence brought a tingle of excitement with it.

As if it were only yesterday she could recall exactly how to reach the Villa Jazmin. Not part of the holiday complex, it was more isolated, much older, he'd told her, going back in time to his grandmother's day when it had been part of his family's large estate. He had described it to her so vividly that she'd had no difficulty in picturing it in her mind's eye, as she had wondered a little wistfully if he would ever suggest that she walked with him along the twisting sandy track to see it in all its summer glory. Perhaps in time he would have done so as their acquaintanceship deepened into the friendship it had promised to become, but something—she still didn't know what—had prevented that from happening.

It had been two weeks before her planned return to England when Merle had taken her customary stroll along the long silver beach to their usual meeting place to find it deserted. Even now she could remember the hollow feeling of disappointment she'd experienced as she had gazed fruitlessly along the beach. It had been irrational in its intensity, but she had cast it aside, consoling herself that Rico's absence must be temporary. If he'd had to leave he would have told her. His courtesy had been one of the most charming qualities about him, and she was sure he had enjoyed their quiet encounters as much as she!

When three days had passed and there had still been no sign of him she had been filled with apprehension, experiencing a feeling of desolation beneath the sheltering pines where once she had found contentment. Suppose he was ill? Or had had an accident and had been unable to call for help? Panic had seized her and she had forsaken any qualms about not wishing to intrude, finding her way easily to the villa. It had been locked and deserted.

Merle's disappointment had been a tangible pain. Some sudden summons back to Seville? she had wondered. The remaining days of her holiday had passed without any indication of Rico's whereabouts or the reason for his unexpected departure. At the time she had felt cheated. She had hoped so much to bid him a formal farewell, perhaps even telling him just how much she had appreciated his company for those few hours each afternoon....

Over the turbulent months which had followed her return to her home she had allowed him to fade from her mind. Now his image returned with remarkable clarity, as did the location of the Villa Jazmin.

Her mind was made up. Leaving her suitcase by the wall without a second glance, she began to retrace her steps towards the main track.

Fifteen minutes later she reached her destination, pausing in the archway that confirmed that her memory had not misled her. Pushing aside the thatch of bougainvillaea that covered its perpendicular sides, she was able to make out the small plaque that proclaimed it the entrance to the Villa Jazmin. Better still, she could detect a gleam of light behind the closed shutters!

Merle sent a quick prayer of thanks to her guardian angel. Whoever it was in residence, the very fact that she knew the owner should prove her veracity and enable her to use the phone to summon transport to take her to a hotel for the night! In the morning things were bound to look better.

Resolutely she walked up the low flight of stone stairs leading to the villa and pushed the bell.

A few seconds passed, then light flooded the interior, blazing out from the window above the sturdy olivewood door. Instinctively Merle held her breath, aware that her heart was thumping painfully behind her ribs. Then the door was opened and Rico de Montilla was staring at her.

He looked hard and sure of himself, a blue open-necked sports shirt tucked into dark closely tailored leather-belted trousers, his black hair thick and well shaped against his proudly sculpted head. Only his eyes were different from the last time she had seen him. Darkly cold and hard as granite, they stared at her with no welcome in their sable depths, while his mouth, which in her memories had been so mobile and tender, was now drawn into a forbidding line.

He had recognised her without doubt, she realised as her insides seemed to wither beneath the coldness of his gaze—and it was painfully clear he wished her a thousand miles away!

'You!' His greeting was terse, his mouth snapping shut into a grim line after the utterance of the monosyllable.

'I'm sorry it's so late,' Merle blurted out unhappily, a wave of embarrassment bringing a flush to her pale skin as she searched for a reason for the iciness of his greeting. Had she interrupted a clandestine lovers' meeting—or even a honeymoon? The months between their last meeting were a blank calendar—anything might have happened in his personal life! 'Or if I'm inter-rupting anything,' she rushed on awkwardly, 'but I've only just got here from the airport and I'm in a spot of trouble. If I could just use your phone?' Her dark blue eyes met the Spaniard's unfriendly regard pleadingly. It was humiliating to beg a favour in the circumstances, but the alternative was even less to her taste.

For a moment Merle thought she would be denied access, then Rico's dark head dipped in acknowledge-ment of her request as he stepped backwards a pace mo-

tioning her to cross the threshold. *'Mi casa es su casa,'*
he told her softly.

Merle felt her cheeks burning as she looked away,
painfully aware of the sarcasm behind his apparent
courtesy. Either she'd come at a grossly inconvenient time
or he harboured some grudge against her of which she
was totally unaware. His whole attitude was so opposed
to what she had expected.... It would have been much
easier to accept that he didn't remember her at all rather
than that he remembered her with such evident dislike!
It was clear from the unspoken message in his sombre
eyes that she was as welcome in his house as a plague
of locusts! In the midst of her distress about her own
predicament she still wished she could erase the icy veneer
which had transfigured what she recalled as being a
warmly attractive face, and had no idea what she should
do.

'You are alone?' he asked coldly as she obeyed his
gesture to enter.

'Yes,' Merle nodded, rushing into speech, in an effort
to lighten the atmosphere. 'You see, I've bought this
holiday villa on the Playa Estate, and I've come here by
myself to look it over: see what decorations it needs
before the summer starts...' She gestured with her slim
hands. 'To organise things generally. Unfortunately my
flight was delayed and it was dark when I arrived,
and——' she gulped as a wave of self-pity engulfed her
'—it looks as if I've been given the wrong key, so I can't
get in!'

'You intend to make a home here?' Rico's gaze drifted
over her with scant regard, a frown creasing his smooth
forehead as she became embarrassingly aware of her
ragged appearance.

'A holiday home,' she agreed, grabbing at the edges
of her blouse and drawing them together as his eyes lin-

gered thoughtfully on her exposed skin. 'We—I—it's such a lovely, unspoiled spot, and I thought when neither I nor my family were here I could let it out.'

'Only now you find yourself unwelcome, *no*?'

'It would appear so, yes.'

Merle didn't like the way he said it, sensing his personal animosity. Dear lord, what had she expected? A year ago, from a chance meeting, an unusual relationship had sprung up between them, almost what one could call a melding of spirits. A strangely satisfying, comforting yet compulsive association—or so, in her innocence, she had imagined! On several occasions she had even sensed a strong pull of physical attraction towards her attractive companion, though she had resolutely denied it.

Each of them had been vulnerable in those balmy summer days, at turning-points in their lives, and each had indulged in a warm, escapist world of sea, sand, sun and philosophical conversation which had exercised and expanded her mind, freeing it momentarily from the weight of sorrow it had borne.

An idea seized her. Did Rico see her return as some kind of threat? Surely he didn't suppose she had any idea of intruding into his life when he was committed elsewhere? The idea was ludicrous, and not worth challenging! She just wished she had a better understanding of men in general—arrogant Spaniards in particular!

She wished, too, that her eyes had been able to deny his attractiveness, her heart been able to control its unexpected agitation, her mind been able to obliterate the memories of the lazy afternoons they had shared together on the beach. Instead she was shocked to admit that their magic had been reawakened at the mere sight of her former companion. Obviously Rico had not been affected in a similar way!

Drawing herself up to her full five feet five inches, Merle regretted her lack of high heels which would at least have brought her eyes to the level of his straight chiselled nose.

'I apologise again for my intrusion. If I could just phone for a taxi to take me to a hotel I needn't bother you any more.'

'A taxi at this time of night?' Straight brows furled in amazement. 'You are very optimistic, *querida*. You're not at the airport now, and as for staying at a hotel, I doubt you'd be welcome without some luggage!'

'But I have luggage!' she assured him eagerly, deciding to ignore his sarcastic endearment. 'I left my case outside the Villa Paraiso.'

'And who is going to retrieve it at this hour, in the dark?' He smiled without humour, his enigmatic eyes boring into her startled gaze. 'You or the taxi driver— or did you suppose *I* would be only too eager to act as your porter?'

This wasn't the charming, tender Rico Merle remembered. She was staring at a man without compassion or understanding. Gone was any semblance of the friendship and liking she had imagined had once existed between them. With every exchange of words between them she was forced to accept that, far from being willing to help her, Rico de Montilla was regarding her with barely restrained hostility.

'I'm sorry, I should never have come here...' She turned abruptly, reaching for the door, wanting only to escape from him. Sleeping on the ground would be preferable to exposing herself one moment longer to the frost of his cool reception. Tears of frustration clouded her vision. She had travelled with such high hopes. Was nothing going to go right for her?

'Wait!' A capable hand closed on her arm and she shuddered at the power of his touch. 'Perhaps you're right. But now you *are* here you must stay. There is a spare room and ample bedclothes available. In the morning you'll tell me where your estate agent is, and I will drive you to him. Doubtless he'll be able to provide you with the correct key. Tonight there's nothing to be done.'

'I can't stay here!' The chilliness of his reception had excluded that solution. She might be destitute, but her pride was the equal of his any day!

'You prefer to insult me by refusing my hospitality?'

'If it was genuinely offered I'd accept it,' Merle returned haughtily. 'But you've made it abundantly clear that, for some reason I don't even begin to understand, you find my presence offensive, and I'm afraid I'm too tired to ask you to explain, so it's best that I leave.'

For a few seconds their gazes clashed, then the man's face relaxed, the long curve of his beautiful mouth twisting into a rueful smile.

'I stand suitably rebuked, Merle.' The sound of her name on his tongue for the first time that night was strangely sweet, recalling memories best forgotten. 'Surprise deprived me of my manners. I thought that either my mind was playing me tricks or you were a ghost returned to haunt me!' The hand that had seized her arm relaxed its hold to travel slowly upwards so that the sensitive skilful fingers could touch her cheek.

'Rico...' Astonished, for the first time she mouthed his name, her senses sharpening as she heard the small hiss of satisfaction that escaped his lips. He was so close to her that she could feel his body warmth, sense the aroma of his skin. With an effort she controlled the mad impulse to raise her hands to his head and drag her fingers through the thick straight ebony of his lustrous hair. What fantasy—half dream, half nightmare—was possessing her?

A year ago she had taken temporary refuge in an illusory world. It would be a terrible mistake to recreate it. Now she had passed through her proverbial vale of tears she must face up to reality—whatever it was and wherever she would find it, but logic told her it could never be here, or with this clever, brooding Spaniard whose aura had fleetingly touched and brightened her life, even if he were to show any desire to re-cultivate their acquaintanceship. They had been platonic friends, that was all. Against all the evidence of her racing senses—that had been all! Tiredness and apprehension were taking their toll of her, that was the obvious explanation.

Parting her lips, gazing up pleadingly into the dark pools of Rico's eyes, she begged silently to be released, not only from his grasp but from the spell he held her in.

'Ah, Merle...' It was no more than a sigh as, incredibly, his mouth covered hers, homing on its soft, trembling outline with a purpose that stupefied her into immobility. It was a lover's kiss, deeply penetrating, ruthlessly possessing. Bewildered by this first ever intimate contact with Rico's body, Merle was left stunned and shaking, gasping when he released her, her hands scrabbling at his chest, trying to push him away, alerted to the anger simmering behind his unwarranted action and the threat it posed her: but worse than that, frightened by the perverse response of her own body to the male assault upon it.

'Ah, Merle...' An intense whisper this time as her hands were pushed aside and his fingers fleetingly touched the pale swell of her breasts, visible between the edges of her tattered blouse as she fought to regain

control over her feelings. 'There was a time when I would
have given you everything I possessed for the pleasure
of taking you to my bed and loving you, losing my body
in your heated depths, taking you and binding myself
to you. I was entranced by you...and you knew that,
didn't you, my dark angel?'

Astounded by the passion echoing in his velvet tones,
and the hard glitter of his narrowed eyes, Merle stood
silent, her breathing light and shallow as her pulse raced.
Of course she had known he liked her, found her a compatible companion, but she had never guessed the depth
of the desire he was admitting, the agony his tortured
voice was laying claim to.

'No, it's not true...' she protested faintly, but he
brushed her words aside, continuing as if she had never
interrupted.

'Did you guess it all, *querida*? Did some instinct warn
you that day by day, hour by hour I was falling into your
trap? That you had created an illusion I would not be
able to resist?'

He took a pace backwards from her, thrusting his
hands into the pockets of his closely tailored black
trousers, his face shuttered, his eyes veiled by the sweep
of jet lashes. 'I was going to ask you to be my
enamorada, mi amante—you understand?'

'Rico, please...that can't be true! I'd only just met
you. We were little more than strangers! You'd never
touched me...' Her widened eyes beseeched him to tell
her he was exaggerating, but her protest was waved away
with an impatient gesture.

'What is time but a passage of the sun? I thought I
knew you: fooled myself that what your lips didn't say
I could read in your eyes—in your actions.' He was
flailing himself with his own scorn, laughing at his own
gullibility. 'I'd convinced myself that you were in-

nocent, untouched, something rare and beautiful...' His
mouth turned in self-mocking humour. 'But you are
right—we were strangers with nothing in common other
than shared tastes in unimportant things, our ethics as
totally distanced as the poles!'

'I had no idea...' White-faced, Merle shook her head,
shocked at her own blindness, but it was as if he had
never heard her murmured interruption as, scalpel-sharp,
his deep voice continued,

'Forgive me if I choose not to believe you, *querida*!
Your act was too carefully planned and played not to be
convincing and too cruel not to deserve punishment. And
as you see, it worked. Too well, in fact, because, fired
with enthusiasm and the thought of conquest, I broke
my own rules of seeking seclusion. I left the solitude of
this place and went to the hotel where you'd told me
you were staying with your friends...'

'Oh, no!' The nerves of Merle's stomach clenched,
precipitating her into a state of nausea, as she realised
with an icy dread what must have happened. At last she
knew why Rico had disappeared from her life without
a word.

'Oh, yes, *querida*!' Contempt sharpened his gaze and
turned his strong jawline into steel, as he continued re-
morselessly, 'I'd decided the time had come to put our
relationship on a more intimate footing. Afternoons were
no longer enough. Damn your friends—my need for your
company was greater than theirs! I intended to ask you
not to return at your usual time that day, but to come
back here with me. We would have dinner together—I'd
bought the food and wine, everything was prepared...and afterwards...' He paused, his eyes blazing
pools of accusation in his taut face.

If only she dared speak, but what could she say? Merle
fought a sudden faintness that made the room grow

darker. Rico was systematically and painfully exposing his own weaknesses, lacerating his own pride in front of her in an act of self-immolation as courageous as it was heartbreaking, and there was no comfort she dared offer.

As if from a great distance she heard his voice continue, deep, husky with emotion, as she closed her eyes, unable to bear the scorn that had turned his face into a mask of condemnation.

'I went to Reception and asked if you were still in the hotel. The Señorita Merle Costain...that's whom I asked for—and do you know what I was told?'

Merle's ashen face told him that she did, as relentlessly he concluded without waiting for her to comment—even if she had been able to find the ability to do so.

'I was told that the *Señora* David Costain was outside on the hotel patio enjoying the delights of the swimming-pool—in the company of her husband and baby daughter!'

CHAPTER TWO

'YOU'RE not laughing...' Rico's eyebrows lifted in mocking invitation. 'I thought it was a good joke, one that would appeal to your sense of humour—*no*? A young woman, married to a much older man, confined to domesticity by the arrival of a child, is taken on holiday, and while her less active husband is resting in the afternoons with their toddler she seeks her own diversion on the beach, regardless of the damage her irresponsibility could cause.'

Merle winced as the cold words hit her like slaps. This was the last way she would ever have wished him to discover her background. There was too much truth in his angry accusation for her to deny it, but there *had* been extenuating circumstances for the silence she had kept.

Meeting Rico's baleful regard, she knew with a sinking heart that this was no time to tell him the kind of marriage she and David had shared. Not only would such an explanation take time, but she would have to be in the right mood and the atmosphere would have to be sympathetic for her to be able to unburden herself. With Rico regarding her with such deeply ingrained contempt she would never find the words which, if they didn't exonerate her actions, might at least make them understandable...

'And there I was....' he continued softly, bitterness cloaking every word '...convinced that you were as virtuous as you were beautiful, behaving like some gauche teenager, fooling myself that heaven itself had planned our meeting—when all the time you belonged to another man!' He shrugged expressive shoulders, not waiting for her reply as his cruel gaze glinted over her. 'Absurd, isn't it? I suppose I should be grateful that I discovered what you were up to in time to deny you the opportunity of giving your husband the horns of the cuckold to wear!' His fingers stabbed at his forehead in a gesture that was frighteningly evocative before he rammed his hands in his pockets and glared at her, his body tall and forbidding, his face as stern as any inquisitor's.

There was a short strained silence as Merle hesitated, her lips parted slightly from the shock of his indictment, guilt washing over her like a wave of pain. She just hadn't been prepared for this confrontation and in her present emotionally drained state she was finding it hard to cope with.

'I thought there was no harm in seeing you in the afternoons,' she said awkwardly at last, wishing desperately that his cold stare wasn't making her feel unclean. It wasn't as if David had ever monitored her actions. As far as he was concerned she had been a free agent. He had trusted her discretion absolutely, and she had never abused that trust, despite Rico's angry accusations!

With a muffled curse Rico moved away from her. 'Heaven help you if you'd been my wife! Day or night I would have demanded your loyalty.' His dark eyes narrowed calculatingly. 'What kind of wife ignores the existence of her husband and her child? *Dios*, you didn't even wear a wedding-ring, did you, you little *coqueta*?'

Despite her lack of Spanish Merle could see from Rico's expression that his description wasn't intended to be flattering, and she had no difficulty in guessing its meaning. There was little point in trying to defend herself, since it was obvious she had been judged and found guilty. And the truth was, she *was* culpable in having given a corner of her heart to this angry foreigner, although at the time she hadn't even realised it.

Faced now with Rico's disdain, how could she explain that she had never deliberately intended to flirt with anyone and that her ring had been discarded because of a sand abrasion beneath it? Besides, the likelihood of his believing her was negligible, and the thought of his calling her a liar as well as a cheat was more than she could bear in her heightened mood of tension.

Instead she swallowed the lump of chagrin that had risen to her throat and made a show of moving her shoulders in a poor display of sang-froid. 'If anything I did misled you, then I'm sorry,' she said quietly.

'Sorry!' he echoed sharply, taking a step towards her and seizing her shoulders in a relentless grip. 'What for, Merlita? For all your sins of omission? For letting me believe you were on holiday with friends? Friends!' He gave a harsh laugh, his breath rasping as he pulled away to stare into her upraised face. 'A husband and a child! *Por Dios!* At first I didn't believe it. I went outside to see for myself—and there you were. The three of you. You, a man old enough to be your grandfather and the child!'

Merle shuddered. David had been in his late fifties, but his illness had aged him beyond his years. 'I would have told you, if I'd had any idea...' she began miserably, her assumed air of insouciance unable to prevail against the sharpness of his assault as she wondered how she could possibly expect him to understand how she had felt. How part of the joy of being with him had been the opportunity of leaving all her pain and anxiety behind her for those few magic hours each day.

'What stopped you, then?' Rico asked sharply, his fingers achingly tight on her flesh. 'Was it because you sensed that if I'd suspected for one moment that you belonged to another man I would never have willingly set eyes on you again?' He shook her gently, insisting on a reply. 'Did you enjoy making a fool out of me? Is playing dangerous games the way you get your kicks, and was I just one more scalp you intended to hang on your belt of holiday romances?'

How could he be so cruel? For a few seconds Merle closed her eyes, blotting out the image of his censorious face, frighteningly aware that behind the anger there lay a fine line of unwilling sexual tension, and that her own nervous system was responding to it.

'Well?' Rico prompted softly. 'I'm waiting for your answer, Merle. Are you unfaithful by nature—or was I an exception?'

'Does it matter?' She faced up to him coolly. 'Whatever my reasons for not being entirely frank with you, you discovered my secret. Isn't that enough for you?'

'Not if you and your family are going to spend part of the summer here in future,' he told her grimly. 'I have every man's sense of self-preservation. Apart from anything else, I want to know if your husband ever found out about your afternoon excursions.'

'For heaven's sake, you make it sound as if I was spending my time in a lover's bed, instead of sitting on a beach!' Merle had hoped to ridicule him, but failed to disturb his cool countenance. With a sigh of exasperation she told him what he wanted to know. 'I can assure you you've no need to worry on that account!' Her lips twisted in a wry grimace; Rico could hardly guess how ironic such a question was. 'David had no idea I was seeing you. I didn't consider our meetings important enough to mention.' She paused, aware that his eyes had darkened with disbelief. 'I enjoyed your company. It was as simple as that. I thought we were just friends. I had no idea you...' She stopped, confused.

'Desired you?' he finished caustically. 'You surprise me, Merle. I'd assumed you realised that although my body was scarred its virility remained intact.'

Stunned by the bitterness in the words, Merle felt the strength of argument drain away from her, as Rico made a small sound of disgust and allowed his hands to drop from her arms.

'I suppose I should be grateful for the lesson you taught me,' he added dourly. 'Never again shall I mistake a passing physical attraction, a basic chemical reaction, for something of greater significance. So perhaps I should be thanking you for the experience instead of berating you!'

'Perhaps you should!' His dismissal of any true feeling for her was strangely hurtful, prompting Merle to utter a more spirited reply. 'To be honest, I find your reaction a little naïve. Just because a woman is married it doesn't mean she can't enjoy the company of other men, surely?' Her small rounded chin rose defiantly. 'I can assure you I never had any intention of being unfaithful to my husband, just because I chose not to disclose his existence. It seems to me your responses to a casual female contact were triggered a little too easily!' As a threatening glint narrowed the dark eyes glowering at her, she went on hurriedly, 'Obviously it was a mistake, my coming here for help, so I'll say *adios* . .'

'*Hasta la vista*, don't you mean?' Rico smiled without humour. 'Since you and your husband are to be my neighbours we're bound to meet again from time to time.'

Merle nodded curtly. The sooner she left the Villa Jazmin the better. Let Rico de Montilla continue to believe for the time being that David would be joining her later. With her reputation in his eyes sunk to rock-bottom, this was no time to tell him that David had died a few months after their return to England, that she had always known his time was limited and that her grief at his loss was total and genuine, although she had never loved him—nor he her.

To her annoyance tears sprang to her eyes as she reached for the doorknob. Surreptitiously she dabbed at them with the back of her hand, knowing they were as much due to tiredness and frustration as they were to David's death. If what she had been brought up to believe was right, her late husband was reunited with the only woman he had truly loved, while her own problems were still manifold!

'Wait!' Rico's peremptory order stopped her. Turning, Merle saw that his face was now devoid of expression, not even a flicker of his previous scorn etched on the pleasant features with their trace of Moorish heritage.

'Now that we understand each other I propose we act in a civilised way. I've offered you a room. I suggest you take it.'

Merle felt her pulse quicken alarmingly. 'That's quite impossible after what you've been saying to me!'

'Indeed not!' He allowed his gaze to dwell on the gap between the edges of her blouse with deliberate impertinence. 'I thought I'd made it quite clear that, despite what I may once have imagined I felt for you, I am no longer tempted by anything you have to offer—however charmingly it is displayed.' His mouth curved in a slight smile as her hands rose to conceal the exposed cleavage with a quick angry movement. 'I've made many mistakes in my life, but one I will never repeat is to have an affair with a married woman! So you'll be able to rest easily in your bed.'

Merle's blue eyes, still bright with unshed tears, met and held Rico's steady gaze. His offer had been made in the most humiliating terms, yet what real option did she have? It was all very well standing on her dignity and rushing out into the night, but the beach wasn't the most comfortable place to sleep, Neither could she be certain of finding help elsewhere. On the other hand, her mouth still tingled from Rico's angry salute when both her mind and body had been forcibly reminded of his hard strength. Without conscious thought her tongue touched the full lower sweep of her lips, as she remembered the intensity of his unwanted tribute.

Even while she stared back at him, her eyes dazed with the need to make the right decision, she saw his expression sharpen with recognition of her dilemma, feeling the colour flood her face as he pre-empted her protest.

'Don't be alarmed, Merlita... I have no intention of poaching on another man's property. As far as I'm concerned the grass on the other side of the fence is trampled and unattractive.'

She was mad to taunt him, but his air of self-righteousness, however justified it might be, was as infuriating to her as was his scornful action of turning her name into the Spanish affectionate diminutive as he looked down his beautiful Andalusian nose at her. 'From the way you acted a few minutes ago I could be forgiven for questioning that statement!' Her eyes spat fire at him.

'You mean because I kissed you?' Eyebrows arched in elegant disbelief. 'But my dear Merle, surely you realised that was merely an experiment to discover how you would react to me after such a long absence? Put it down to research rather than the pursuit of pleasure. I wanted to know just how fickle you could be.'

'Then I hope you were satisfied!' For the life of her she couldn't remember how she had reacted to his sudden assault. On top of everything else it had been just too much. A cold shiver of trepidation travelled down her spine. For all she knew his declaration of a past desire for her was total fabrication, his sole purpose being to discomfit her, to punish her in his own coin for the actions he saw as breaking his own strict code of morality.

His glance raked over her, missing nothing, from the challenging tilt of her head to the way her fingers trembled slightly against her breast.

He nodded. 'Enough to repeat my assurances that you will be as safe under my roof as you would be in a nunnery. And now we understand each other may I offer you some refreshment before we start getting your room ready?'

Wary and uncomfortable, Merle allowed him to lead her through an archway into what appeared to be the main sitting-room. On two levels joined by two further archways, it was a large, pleasant room with a polished flagstone floor, simple olivewood furniture and two splendidly opulent leather couches. A large stone fireplace was occupied by a metallic urn amply filled with fresh flowers, while the alcoves in the white stone walls contained a selection of elegant bric-à-brac.

At Rico's invitation she sank gratefully down on one of the couches, murmuring her acceptance of a cup of coffee but refusing anything to eat. The meal served on the flight had been adequate in the circumstances—any resurging appetite having abated as a result of the heated confrontation with her host.

The coffee when he brought it was accompanied by a large brandy.

'Oh, I don't think...' Merle began doubtfully.

'Drink it.' Rico drew out the smallest from a nest of tables, placing it before her and resting the glass and cup on it. 'One glass of Fundador never hurt anyone, and you look as if you need it.'

'All right, thank you.' She gave him a tentative smile. 'Doctor's orders?'

'If you like.' He regarded her solemnly before reaching in his pocket and holding out his lean-fingered hand, palm up towards her. 'I thought you might like to have this, to effect running repairs.' Nestling on the smooth masculine skin was a slim gold tie-pin with a hooped head of seed pearls and tiny sapphires.

His eyes, a dark oloroso now in the subdued light of the wall-lit room, rested for a moment on where one of Merle's hands still held the torn edge of her blouse in place.

'Thank you.' She was touched by his thoughtfulness, although a plain safety-pin would have been more suitable for the purpose of retaining her modesty! 'I'll let you have it back as soon as I can get my case and change.'

'There's no hurry.' Rico waved aside her thanks, choosing to sit opposite her, holding his own glass of brandy and stretching long muscled legs out into the space between them, as she slid the pin into the gaping cotton edges at her breasts, before shrugging off the jacket which had been inadequate to cover her revealed skin.

He'd changed in the last twelve months, she thought, her task completed, sipping the heady spirit in her glass. There seemed to be a new maturity, a greater serenity and less strain in the face which she remembered as being more than usually attractive even then. She wondered if life had been good to him and found herself unexpectedly hoping that it had.

'Did you get the position you were after last year at the clinic in Cadiz? she asked hesitantly, half afraid that he wouldn't be prepared to discuss his personal life with her, yet strangely anxious to know if he had been successful.

To her relief, he nodded. 'So you remember that, do you?'

'That you were hoping to join them as an orthopaedic surgeon?' Merle was momentarily hurt that he could think her interest in him had been so shallow that she could possibly have forgotten what had been so obviously important to him. 'Of course I remember. I often wondered if your application had been successful and how it worked out.'

'I was lucky,' he admitted, his broad frame appearing to lose some of its previous tension. 'The board considered my experience in the field more than compensated for my lack of years.'

Merle shivered, remembering how Rico's field experience had nearly cost him his life in Nicaragua when he had been caught in crossfire between two groups of combatants, while trying to save an injured woman. The machine-gun bullets which had splayed within a hair's breadth of his spine had left a diagonal tracing of angry seared flesh from his left shoulder-blade to just above the right side of his lean waist, as a lasting memento.

That first day she'd met him she had wandered far along the seemingly endless stretch of silver beach, leaving the hotels in the distance, deeply immersed in her thoughts, enjoying the rush of the cool Atlantic against her feet, when she had realised how hot the sun had become on the top of her uncovered head. Shade in that part was at a premium, but she had espied a cluster of pine trees way back where the beach met with scrubland and what appeared to be the beginning of a path.

Thankfully she had ploughed her way through the soft sand, only realising when she was a few yards away that the area wasn't deserted as she'd believed but that a man was seated there, back against one of the trees, reading: long tanned legs emerging in beautiful male musculature from short white shorts and a flimsy short-sleeved cotton shirt hinting at an equally well-developed torso between its open edges knotted at his lean waist.

As Merle had approached he had looked up and in response to her uncertain smile had invited her to share his shade, speaking first in Spanish and then, as he saw her struggling to translate the words, doing the job for her and repeating them again in flawless English.

She hadn't been too surprised he had discerned her nationality. When foreigners realised that her dark hair had Gaelic red rather than Latin blue undertones it seldom took them long to work out that her flawless magnolia skin owed its perfection to the notoriously damp air of the British Isles!

Thus Rico de Montilla had entered her life at one of its lowest ebbs. There had been something about him which had drawn her back time and again, something she hadn't wanted to stop and analyse, as each day when David and Laurie took their long afternoon siestas together she had traced her footsteps back to the welcoming shade of the pine trees and the pleasure of Rico's company.

It was two weeks after their first meeting that she had been delayed because Laurie had been fretful and she had stayed to soothe her, despite David's assurances that he could perfectly well cope with his three-year-old daughter. The space beneath the trees had been deserted as Merle's heart had plummeted painfully, a real sense of loss spreading through every cell of her body at Rico's absence. It was then she should have been warned how dangerously warm her feelings for this engaging Andalusian had become, but somehow the knowledge had eluded her. She had always imagined that love for her would be a slow process as liking grew into love over many months. She'd never expected it to be born and mature like a may-fly in a matter of hours!

Sinking down on the soft sand, using the full turquoise seersucker skirt she wore over her one-piece swimsuit as a barrier against the sand, she had barely settled herself down when, turning her attention to the sea, she saw a figure emerging from it. Her heart had seemed to perform impossible acrobatics as a weird yawning ache spread uncertain tentacles through her nervous system to touch every muscle of her body.

She'd told herself her reaction was due to mild heat-stroke, but watching Rico come lazily towards her, his strong graceful body so aggressively balanced, his shirt hooked over one shoulder, she knew *he* was responsible for this inexplicable thing that was happening to her...

'I thought you weren't coming!' His pleasure at seeing her had been so intense she could almost feel it warming her skin. Laughingly she had risen to her feet, going towards him as he had held out his hands to her. The next moment she'd been in his arms, his flesh cold and damp but incredibly exciting against her, her hands reaching for his back, touching his naked skin, feeling the raised pattern of scarred tissue that marred the oilskin smoothness of the surrounding tissue.

She had heard his intake of breath and let her hands fall, terrified that she had hurt him, but the pain in his dark searching eyes had not been physical as he had asked her tautly, 'You find my *cicatriz* repulsive, Merlita? To be honest, I had wished to hide it from you for a while longer.'

He had swung round, presenting to her eyes the sight of which only her fingers had knowledge. Merle had gazed her fill, absorbing with every sense of her body the splendid mature frame before her, her eyes registering the smoothly developed muscles of his shoulders, the sleekly sculptured line of his ribs, the faintest trace of dark hair at the narrowest part of his torso where the golden skin disappeared into his dark bathing trunks.

The scars weren't disfiguring—even if she hadn't felt her heart swell with sympathy for him she would have been able to look at them without flinching. Like a primitive tribal decoration their half-hoop served to highlight the smooth perfection of their background. For a fleeting moment Merle marvelled at his self-consciousness, then her natural compassion took over from her inherent shyness.

'Repulsive?' she had heard her own voice crack a little. 'How could anything about you ever be repulsive?' It had been the point where things had begun to go badly wrong, only then in her innocence she truly hadn't realised it. Rico de Montilla had been a fully mature man approaching his thirtieth birthday, and every fibre of her mind and body had been forced to recognise that fact!

Somehow she had managed to blank the realisation from her consciousness, making an effort to drain the tension from the charged atmosphere by encouraging Rico to confide his experiences in South America, listening with rapt attention as he had told her how on a visit to see his mother in Argentina he had met relief workers from Nicaragua and learned from them the need for skilled medical help.

'It was a challenge,' he had explained quietly. 'I'd qualified and specialised in Spain as an orthopaedic surgeon and had every intention of returning there—but first...' He had opened his palms upward in a gesture of despair. 'It was a call I couldn't refuse. I'd been there just over a year when I got caught in crossfire—and this was the result.'

Looking back, Merle could see how her own confused feelings had deceived Rico, yet at the time she had truly thought his interest in her had been compounded of curiosity, the pleasure he took in perfecting his English and the loneliness his chosen isolation during convalescence had visited on him.

Merle's hand shook slightly as she drained the glass of brandy, placing it on the table beside the now empty coffee-cup, aware that during the past few moments of silence Rico's eyes had been fastened to her face. He looked thoughtful rather than haughty now, and she wondered what he had read there; she hoped it was her regret that she had ever given him cause to condemn her!

When a few minutes later he suggested that she might like to go to her room, she followed him up the open-plan staircase to a small room containing a single bed with an intricately carved olivewood headboard, a low dressing table in similar wood and a free-standing wardrobe which was obviously part of the suite.

'The bathroom's next door.' Rico indicated the direction with a brief nod of his dark head, leaving her alone to accustom herself to her surroundings before returning with an armful of white linen.

'I've got an apartment in Cadiz,' he told her conversationally, shaking a sheet over the mattress with a show of domestic skill which surprised her. 'Actually it's in the grounds of the clinic itself, but I find this place very convenient for a relaxing break, especially as it's equidistant from my work and my brother's *cortijo*. One of the local women comes in on a daily basis while I'm here and keeps the place tidy and the fridge stocked as well as doing the laundry, so I'm quite prepared for the unexpected guest.'

'So I see.' Glad that their conversation had achieved an impersonal civility, Merle reached for one of the pillows Rico had placed on the dressing-table, slipping it inside the cover he had provided. 'I still feel dreadful, imposing on you like this. If I could have thought of any alternative....' She stopped, aware that her implication was scarcely flattering, yet not meaning to be offensive.

'Not at all.' His dark regard showed no emotion. 'You were in an unfortunate predicament. Whatever our differences I should have felt more offended by your decision not to come here than by your arrival—although I admit I was more shaken to see you than I had supposed would be the case.' It was a smooth statement and just for a moment Merle wondered how seriously he had considered the possibility of meeting her again, before he asked politely, 'Will you be warm enough with just this cover over the sheet?'

It was a thick blue and white woven spread which he had draped across the bed. Beneath it Merle knew she would find the warmth and comfort her body craved.

'Thank you. That will be ample.'

Rico made her a stiff formal bow, eyes shuttered, long lashes a fan against his high Andalusian cheekbones. 'In that case I'll wish you *buenas noches*.' For a moment she saw the shadow of a smile soften his firm masculine mouth. 'I regret I'm unable to provide you with night attire. My guests usually bring their own—should they require it.' He paused fractionally as if inviting her to consider the kind of guests he might invite who would consider nightwear extraneous to their needs. It wasn't a difficult vision to conjure up. Rico de Montilla was a highly charged male animal. In the past David's existence as her husband had acted as a screen between that knowledge and the full realisation of its potency. With that screen removed her perception had sharpened to a painful and unwelcome intensity.

She watched him leave the room, waiting for the sound of his footsteps to fade as he went downstairs before leaving the room to enter the bathroom, glad that she had a small selection of toilet things in her shoulder-bag. At least she could wash and clean her teeth in an effort to restore her morale!

The sheets were cool to her naked body as she slid beneath them, their crispness scented with a heady perfume that owed nothing to modern washing powders but everything to the way they had been aired in the hot Spanish sunlight. An evocative mixture of myrtle and sweet basil that was as effective as any soporific prescribed by a doctor.

Tomorrow would see things back to normal, Merle thought as with her own body heat trapped beneath the traditional cover she felt sleep overtake her. Tomorrow she would get the right key from the estate agent and take possession of her new domain. Then, apart from the formal greeting decreed by custom when their paths crossed on their day-to-day business, she need never speak to Rico de Montilla again! They would become the strangers he so obviously wished they were!

CHAPTER THREE

A SHARP rapping at her door accompanied by the delicious smell of freshly brewed coffee awakened Merle the following morning. Stretching luxuriously, she hauled herself upright on the comfortable mattress, instantly aware of her surroundings.

'Come in!' Hastily she arranged the sheet to shield her nakedness as Rico obeyed her summons.

'Did you sleep well?' The question was courteously asked as he placed a cup of coffee on the small table at her side, with nothing in his voice to remind her of the previous day's abrasivenes. Standing back, he appraised her sleep-flushed face, politely awaiting her response.

'Like a baby!' Merle smiled her gratitude stiffly, acknowledging the tenuous armistice between them. 'Last night I was beginning to feel I couldn't cope with the situation, but this morning I feel refreshed enough to face anything.'

'*Bueno* ... Let us hope the problem is easily solved.' Rico turned away from her before she could question what she had detected as a note of reservation in his comment. 'In the meantime I've brought you something you'll be needing.'

He was out of the door, returning in seconds with her suitcase and putting it down at the foot of the bed.

'Oh, marvellous!' Her face lit up with pleasure. 'But how did you find it? I mean, I didn't tell you where my villa was, did I? And I certainly didn't expect you to go out so early in the morning on my behalf.'

Rico shrugged broad shoulders clad this morning in a navy T-shirt above white cotton trousers which seemed to emphasise the lean power of his lower body. 'I know the Playa Estate. It's not that large, and since only one of the villas had a suitcase outside its walls there was no need for supernormal detective powers. As for the time...' he raised lazy shoulders '...it seemed prudent to go early before someone else saw it and interfered. Besides, it's not unusual for me to go for a swim first thing.'

'Oh, I wish I'd known—I would have...' Confused, Merle stopped. For a moment she had forgotten the harsh exchanges of yesterday. Probably the last thing Rico had wanted was her company on an early morning beach outing, despite the present aura of truce he exuded.

'I thought you needed your sleep.' To her relief he ignored the opportunity of embarrassing her by overt rejection. 'No doubt there'll be many opportunities for you to swim before breakfast in the coming days.'

Had there been an odd inflexion in his voice, or had she imagined the note of doubt in what should have been a reassuring statement? For the second time she felt a strange sense of foreboding. Perhaps he thought her interest in the property was less genuine than she was claiming. In which case he was in for a disappointment.

'Yes, of course I shall,' she retorted firmly. 'Once I've got this matter of the key sorted out it'll only be a matter of days before my family join me here and we can all enjoy the sunshine and sea.'

Rico glanced down at his watch. 'Then the sooner we obtain the right key for you the better. Where exactly do we find this estate agent of yours?'

'Seville.' Leaning out of the bed, Merle drew up her shoulder-bag from its position on the floor, searching in its depths for her purse with one hand while the other anchored the sheet firmly between her breasts, uncomfortably aware of the amusement lurking in the depths of Rico's dark eyes at the contortions necessary to retain her modesty. Let him laugh at her! Yesterday he had called her a *coqueta*. Today she'd give him no cause to repeat the insult.

'Here...' A few seconds later she had retrieved the business card from her purse and offered it to the patiently waiting man at her bedside. 'Perhaps you could phone him on my behalf?' Her azure eyes darkened in supplication. 'As it's his mistake he may be prepared to send someone over here with the right key.'

'Possibly.' Rico took the card from her, casting a cursory glance at it. 'On the other hand, there are one or two things I need in Seville myself, and I always feel a face-to-face confrontation is the best way of solving a problem.'

'Well, if it's not inconveniencing you too much...' If there had been an alternative solution Merle would have taken it, rather than throw herself on Rico's generosity, but it wasn't just for her own peace of mind, she consoled herself: Barbie's family and Laurie were depending on her to deliver the glorious holiday she had promised them. For their sakes she must learn to swallow her pride and to take the easiest way of achieving her purpose.

'Not at all,' Rico informed her gravely. 'A couple of hours by road will see us there, and we can start immediately after breakfast. An acquaintance of mine is one of the chefs at the Majestic Palace, so I called in on my way back along the beach and collected some freshly baked rolls still hot from the oven, so if you like them warm don't be too long in coming down.'

'The Majestic Palace!' Merle's voice echoed her surprise. 'But that's a couple of miles along the beach from here, isn't it? You must have taken a long walk!'

'About five kilometres, I believe.' His dark eyes dwelt on the soft fair skin of her attractive face. 'Let's just say that I was up very early this morning, not having enjoyed the blessing of a long night's sleep, hmm?' He left the room before she could respond.

Thankfully Merle allowed the sheet to drop as she reached for her coffee, drinking it with real pleasure. Had that last remark been loaded? Had her presence irritated Rico to the extent of depriving him of sleep? She replaced her cup and with unaccustomed annoyance thumped her pillow. Damn that stupid estate agent for sending her the wrong key! If it hadn't been for his inefficiency she would have been spared this embarrassment!

Thankful at least that her small but adequate wardrobe had been returned to her, she scrambled out of bed, unlocked the case and extracted the pink satin sleeveless nightshirt she'd packed. Clad in this, she gained the bathroom, returning a few minutes later showered and lightly made-up, her dark hair brushed away from her smooth forehead and held in place by a white chiffon scarf. Selecting the briefest of cotton underclothes on her return, she replaced the nightshirt with these, topping them with a pastel print skirt and matching short-sleeved bolero over a strapless white top. It was an easy outfit to wear, cool and formal enough for town but easily transformed into a sun-dress should the opportunity arise.

Despite the edginess she felt in Rico's presence she was filled with a joyous anticipation at the prospect of seeing Seville. Last year David had been too weak to travel far from the hotel, and although he had encouraged her to go by herself on some of the organised tours she had always refused, not wanting to leave him alone for too long. It was ironical that the few hours she had stolen, with his blessing, when he had been resting, had resulted in her being branded a *femme fatale* by a man whose respect she would have welcomed but which had now been irretrievably lost to her!

Sighing, Merle removed a pair of smart new wedge-heeled peep-toe shoes from her case and slid her elegant slender feet into their cushioned comfort. In retrospect she couldn't blame her unwilling host for his scornful judgement on her past behaviour. If she could have the time again she would have been more cautious, but then she was looking at events with the hindsight of experience. There was little doubt she had changed in the months since David had died. The responsibility of being alone, of dealing with the large estate bequeathed to her, of trying desperately to discern and meet the needs of the baby daughter denied the fond affection of a loving father...they had all made their mark on her, ageing her mentally if not physically. No, she was no longer the timorous naïve girl whose heart had warmed so innocently to the charisma of the youngest Montilla brother...

Somewhere she had packed a large, squashy white bag, ideal to complete her outfit. Diligently she searched for it, unwilling to disturb the contents of the case too radically. On her return from Seville she would be transporting it back to the Playa Estate and the Villa Paraiso where it could be completely unpacked. As she felt through the layers of clothes with sensitive fingers her train of thought continued. Undoubtedly Rico, too, had changed. She had met him at a time when he was convalescing physically and emotionally from the horrors of war, the scars on his mind less obvious but potentially more serious than those on his body.

Still uncertain as to whether his confession of having experienced desire for her had been genuine or a means of attacking her, Merle decided that if he had spoken the truth then it had been because he too had been caught in an emotional vacuum—haunted by tragedies that the human mind refused to rationalise. In that state it was only too easy to imagine feelings which had no roots in reality....

She gave a small murmur of satisfaction as her seeking hand closed on the bag and she was able to withdraw it. Yes, Rico had changed. A year ago he had been living the life of a hermit, refusing to stray more than a few yards from the quiet sanctuary of the Villa Jazmin and the nearby beach. Now he had secured an important and worthwhile job and clearly enjoyed the healthiest of minds in the healthiest of bodies.

Leaving the bedroom and making her way downstairs, her mouth watering as the smell of fresh bread titillated her senses, Merle was certain of one thing. However much Rico de Montilla might despise her, she was delighted that he had made a complete recovery from his South American ordeal. Not that for one moment she had ever doubted his ability to do so...

His attitude towards her as they shared the Continental breakfast was beyond reproach. He was polite in the extreme, treating her as an honoured guest with none of the previous evening's hostility apparent. Watching him covertly as he raised his cup to his lips, Merle found it difficult to believe that he had kissed her with such punitive intent or used such evocative words to describe the desire he once claimed to have harboured towards her. There was nothing now in his bearing to suggest that he felt anything other than the need to extend hospitality to a visitor to his country. Aware of his disdain, though, she resented being obligated to him, but maybe that state of affairs would soon be ended!

Leaving the Villa Jazmin immediately after breakfast as he had suggested, they entered the environs of Seville in Rico's small dark Seat, shortly after eleven.

'Not very luxurious, I'm afraid,' he had admitted on opening the passenger door for her at the commencement of their journey. 'But she's ideal for the country roads and easy to park in the city.'

'She looks fine to me!' Merle had been only too grateful for the door-to-door transport, and indeed the journey had been smooth and comfortable as Rico's precision touch on the controls sped them quickly and safely towards their destination.

Her first sight of Seville was disappointing as they entered the city through the hot and dusty industrial outskirts, but as they drew nearer to the centre she cried out in delight as she caught sight of the famous and beautiful landmarks.

'You've never been here before?' Curiously Rico questioned her.

'No.' She was too excited to attempt to hide her happiness. 'Last year was the first time I'd ever come to Spain, and we didn't go far from the beach.' She paused, then added, 'But David, my husband, had been here before. He wanted me to go on one of the tours to Seville, but...' She stopped, unwilling to plunge into the reasons David hadn't taken her, and hoping her unfinished sentence would be allowed to die without comment.

'But you found the pleasures of sea and sand more to your liking, hmm?' A dark eyebrow lifted in her direction. 'That doesn't make you unusual among your compatriots. In fact many of them appear to prefer the inside of bars to the attractions of nature, let alone culture.'

'You don't care for the tourists?' A slight edge to her voice challenged him.

'I try not to generalise.' Rico steered the car neatly into a side-road. 'Their advent has brought prosperity and disaster hand in hand to this country, a state of affairs for which they are not entirely to blame. It is a sad fact of mass tourism that by its very nature it tends to destroy that which it most desires to enjoy. En masse it would be fair to say I resent them. Individually,' he slid her a sideways glance, 'individually I find some compatible.' He made another turn, this time steering the car neatly into a private forecourt and bringing it to a halt. 'This is the address you gave me.'

The estate agent's was in a small modern block of buildings, its large window filled with colourful photographs of villas. Obviously a company which catered for the influx of tourists rather than the domestic market, Merle thought wryly. In which case she should have no difficulty in making her complaint known.

'I can manage now, thank you.' She turned to Rico as he came to join her at the window. 'I'm sure someone there will speak English if you want to go and do your own business.'

'There's no hurry.' To her surprise he placed a firm hand beneath her elbow, preparing to shepherd her into the office. 'I have to collect a watch that's in for repair, that's all, so we'll get this problem settled first. It's always possible you may need my help.'

He couldn't have spoken a truer word, Merle ruefully agreed some ten minutes later when the young woman to whom she had put her complaint continued to insist that there had been no mistake.

'We sent you the key to the Villa Paraiso,' she said positively, her dark eyes showing annoyance at Merle's persistence. 'I can assure you, *señora*, there has been no mistake!'

'But it doesn't fit!' Merle felt as if she were losing her reason. In exasperation she turned to bring a silently watchful Rico into the battle. 'You tell her, please, Rico! You know I couldn't have made a mistake!'

Opening her bag, she seized her purse, intent on thrusting the evidence before the girl.

'The *señora* is correct,' Rico confirmed calmly. 'I tried the key myself. There is no way it fits.' His hand slid into the pocket of his close-fitting trousers, reappearing with the key between his fingers and pushing it across the counter towards the clerk.

So he hadn't trusted her judgement! This morning when he had gone to collect her case he must have taken her key and tried the lock himself, which meant he had come into her bedroom while she slept... It had been warm in the early hours of the morning and she had allowed the covers to drift down her body... Had Rico looked at her half-naked body—or had he been too involved in his purpose to have spared her a glance? A wave of embarrassment flowed through her. Stoically she ignored it, dwelling rather on the fact that at least he was in a position to corroborate her declaration.

'Then the lock must have been changed!' The clerk's liquid eyes dwelt on Rico's face, their impatience masked with a new kind of respect. 'I do assure you, *señora*——'

'I think you may be right.' Tersely he interrupted her, as Merle asked in shocked surprise,

'Changed? How could it have been changed? No one had the authority to change it——'

'Hush! There is nothing to be obtained by arguing the point here.' Rico's arm fastened securely on her own, guiding her from the premises as he murmured a polite farewell to the intrigued clerk.

'What do I do now?' Furiously Merle detached her arm from his grasp, turning to face him beneath the blazing sunshine of the street.

'You tell me who has the deeds of the property.'

'The solicitor who acted for the vendors.' Fighting to control the way her fingers were shaking, Merle took her purse from her bag, extracting a business card. 'Here it is—Señor Juan Montero. We arranged that I should collect them from his office here in Seville on my arrival.'

'Let me see.' Rico took the card from her hand, perusing it thoughtfully. 'How very convenient! His office is quite close to where we are. We'll find a phone and I'll see if I can make an appointment to see him.'

'You think he may have the right key?' Merle asked eagerly, a ray of hope illuminating the gloom that had descended on her.

But she was to receive no answer as Rico discerned a phone available for public use and moved swiftly from her side. Minutes later he was back, his expression quietly triumphant.

'He'll see us at four o'clock.'

'Not until then?' Dismay was mirrored in her widened eyes, as Rico greeted her protest with a wry twist of his mouth.

'Consider yourself lucky. We Andalusians, more than anyone else in Spain, use the philosophy of *mañana*. In truth, he originally suggested some time the week after next.'

Rebuked, Merle had the grace to feel ashamed. 'Forgive me, I wasn't complaining on my own behalf, but you'll be wanting to get back to the coast.'

'Not at all.' He glanced at the thin gold watch on his wrist. 'I intend to stay with you until we get this matter clear. In the meantime I suggest we stroll through the streets towards the Jardines del Alcázar. On the way I can collect my other watch. We should then have time to visit the Cathedral and the Giralda Tower, by which time we should be ready for lunch.' He shrugged his shoulders. 'By the time we've eaten, our appointment will be due.' His quizzical look invited her approval of his plan.

There was nothing she could do but nod her acceptance, although his generosity put her even further under his obligation.

'This way, then.' Acknowledging her rather subdued agreement, Rico guided her gently across the road, one hand lightly on her arm, moving with a positive masculine grace which suggested he had never considered her disputing his plans.

Later, walking through the ancient quarter of the city, Merle was glad she had raised no objection to the sight-seeing tour. This was the Andalusia of her dreams: the Spain that David had enthused about. In the midst of an urban city here was an enclave of haunting beauty— a glistening maze of white houses and narrow alleys, where a myriad flowers spilled from wrought-iron balconies in a riot of colour and perfume. It was dramatic and beautiful, a picture painted in bold tones of white and scarlet and black where the deep shadows contrasted against the glare of the whitewashed walls.

'I feel as if I'm on a stage set,' she confided, her lingering concern about the coming interview temporarily diverted by her surroundings.

'It struck me that way too, when I first came here.' Rico smiled slightly, turning his head to meet her sparkling eyes. 'Even now I can never take it for granted like the people who were born here. I still see it with the admiring eyes of a stranger.'

'Of course,' Merle remembered what he had once told her in the days when they had enjoyed each other's company, 'you were born in Argentina, weren't you?'

'Uh-huh, but my father was Andalusian. I lived over there until I was seventeen, then I came back to Spain to live with my brother Armando and study for the medical profession. So you see, although I have the blood of Andalusia in me, I still see her through the eyes of a visitor.'

'Is that good or bad?' There'd been something behind the coolness of his expression that prompted her enquiry.

'Who knows?' Rico made a careless gesture with both hands. 'It means I perceive her beauty more sharply but by the same criterion am less inured to her ugliness. It's not always a comfortable relationship.'

There was a flash of anger in the dark eyes which met her own, a return of the previous hostility with which he had first greeted her, as if it was she to whom he was referring rather than the city; then it was gone, leaving her feeling oddly bereft, and he was leading her towards a gracious forecourt where canopied tables invited the hot and weary traveller to rest.

Sipping gratefully at a fresh iced orange juice, Merle leaned back against the padded headrest of her wrought-iron chair, her eyes fastening on Rico's lean handsome face. There was, she thought, a special quality about him that didn't depend on the almost classical beauty of his features with their obvious debt to his Moorish ancestry, a mingling of composure and authority in his bearing that gave maturity to a face of hard bones and cleanly cut sweeping curves. If it came to a fight he was a man she would want on her side, despite the disquieting air of antagonism which was never far below the surface of his stylised courtesy.

Last year she had seen the handsome Spaniard as a fellow spirit: someone with whom she could relax and discuss shared likes and interests. Now, because of his denunciation of what he saw as her wilful deceit and betrayal of her husband's trust, he seemed tougher, more formidable. Oh, how she resented his arbitrary judgement! Was she fated to be the victim of men with shining, rigid consciences? First her stepfather and now Rico? She stole a quick look at her companion's face, knowing she should hate him for his cursory condemnation. And what about his own motives? What was particularly honourable in planning to seduce a woman for a quick, casual summer affair? For that was all it had been.

Suppose she told Rico the truth about her marriage with David—and how it had ended? Would it make him regard her in a kindlier light—make him feel any shame for the way he had treated her yesterday?

She stretched out her legs, turning her closed eyes towards where the sun filtered down between the tables, and decided to hold her peace. Try as she might, it was impossible to forget the passionate persuasion of the contemptuous kiss Rico had inflicted on her the previous evening or her spontaneous response to it. The continued presence of a husband in her life was the best protection she could imagine against Rico's undoubted ability to trample on her bruised emotions.

Inhaling the mingled aromas of deeply scented carnations and the delicious smells from a Spanish kitchen, Merle sighed deeply. Yes, the longer she could pretend she was still a married woman the easier it would be for her to remain aloof from Rico's very personal blend of Latin charm and male machismo. As a guide around Seville he had been both attentive and informative, she reflected wryly, and on the occasions he had taken her

arm or clasped her hand to guide her across the thronging
roads, she'd had to remind herself that his actions were
all a part of his inherent courtesy: that there had been
nothing personal about it. Yet it would have been all
too easy in those magical hours to have fooled herself
into believing she could regain his friendship.

In the circumstances, she reflected, her peace of mind
depended on the preservation of her own pride, rather
than attempting to resurrect the camaraderie which had
been built on such a fragile and specious base!

'What will you eat, Merle?' Her eyes flicked open as
Rico's deep voice penetrated her thoughts.

'I'm really not very hungry...' She took the menu he
offered her, scanning its contents. 'I'm afraid tension
always affects my appetite.' She cast him an apologetic
look, adding for good measure lest he should assume it
was his presence which was disturbing her metabolism,
'And this business about the villa has wound me up.'

'Like an alarm clock.' Dark eyes set in deeply cut
sockets beneath thick straight brows regarded her speculatively while the vestige of a smile dimpled the corner
of his sensuous mouth, as he acknowledged his understanding of her colloquialism. 'Let us hope you are not
about to explode with a shattering peal to disturb the
tranquillity of the afternoon. Since you intend to take
up residence here you will have to learn to live at the
tempo which surrounds you, or you'll end up a very
frustrated young woman.'

'You're talking about the cult of *mañana*.' Merle made
a moue of resignation, irritated by the light mockery of
his tone.

'Ah, you Anglo-Saxons!' The lines at each side of
Rico's mouth deepened in amusement. 'It is you who
waste time, by abusing rather than using it. What is one
day more or less in the scheme of things?'

'A philosophical hypothesis, but one which won't help to get a roof over my head!' Merle decided against pointing out that she was Gaelic rather than Anglo-Saxon, fancying that to a Spaniard it was a moot difference.

'Relax!' He sounded more amused than contrite at her tart retort. 'Since you can't fight the inevitable you may just as well enjoy a leisurely lunch. If it's something light you fancy why not try the *gambas* with a salad? And to drink, tell me, which do you prefer, wine or *sangría*?'

Bowing to the inevitable as recommended, Merle sighed, accepting his suggestion of the large grilled prawns marinated in seasoned oil and served with lemon wedges with a side dish of lettuce, tomatoes, cucumber and olives.

It was then, just as she was beginning to relax beneath the sun's hot caress, that Rico brought her sharply back to reality. Leaning forward to fill her tall glass with the iced *sangría* she had chosen in preference to wine, he said calmly, 'So your husband has chosen to stay at home and look after your daughter?'

His voice had lifted slightly at the end of the sentence, turning it into a question as his eyes caught and held her shocked gaze.

CHAPTER FOUR

MERLE stared back at him, blindingly aware that her bluff was being called. Staunch to her previously determined resolution, she searched her mind for an explanation which would not be entirely untrue.

'He—no——' she stumbled, aware of Rico's keen penetrating brown eyes regarding her with interest. 'David is away—out of the country—that's why I'm handling the business.' That at least was true. David was away in a place not plagued by the sorrows and problems of this life, if what the churches taught was true, she comforted herself, swallowing a sudden surge of unhappiness at the memory of a gentle and compassionate man no longer able to enjoy the sights and sounds that surrounded her at that moment.

'Ah!' Rico sat back in his chair, lifting a prawn from his plate and neatly extricating it from its shell. 'Then your daughter—I don't believe I know her name—your daughter will be staying with your own parents, no doubt.'

'Laurie. Her name is Laurie.' His sudden interest in her family was unexpected and unwelcome. Presumably it was his way of passing the time while they ate. In view of his assistance it would be churlish to resent his questions. She would just have to tread carefully if she were to preserve the myth of her married status! She took a long draught from her glass before completing her reply. 'As a matter of fact she's being looked after by my sister Barbara. She and her husband Grant have a daughter just a year older than Laurie. As soon as I've got the villa organised they'll all be coming over here for a holiday.'

Rico nodded. 'You and your sister are perhaps orphans?'

'No, not at all.' Merle was quick to correct him, feeling on safer ground now David himself had been dropped as a subject. 'My mother and stepfather live in Scotland.'

'Then they will also enjoy a holiday in the Spanish sun, *no*?'

'I'm afraid not.' Merle couldn't keep the regret from her voice. 'I'm sure my mother would love to come over here, but my stepfather never goes on holiday.'

'Perhaps you'll be able to persuade her to come over by herself, then.'

'He'd never allow it!' The bitter words were out before Merle could control them. As usual whenever she thought of her mother, dominated by the man who had married her after she had become a widow and whose possessiveness towards her had made the lives of his stepdaughters a misery, she felt a burning resentment. Latent fury darkened her eyes to ultramarine as she added disparagingly, 'But then you wouldn't find that kind of dictatorial attitude in a man as appalling as I do!'

Rico didn't deny it, but the flash of anger that flickered across his lean features had its origin in another source. 'You consider you know me so well you can forecast my opinions?' he demanded silkily.

Once that would have been true. Now he was a stranger, as potentially explosive as a stick of dynamite.

'If I prejudged you, I'm sorry...' Merle stared down at her plate, knowing her reactions were born of the long-held animosity she had nursed against her stepfather. 'I did assume that, your being Andalusian, your attitude towards women would be one of absolute sovereignty.

But not without evidence, surely?' Her beautiful sweep of dark-winged brows lifted slightly above innocently wide eyes. 'It was only yesterday that you told me you would demand loyalty day or night from your wife!'

'True.' His dark eyes gleamed with a breathtaking arrogance. 'Although I'm not sure that being Andalusian has anything to do with it. Far from being parochial, I consider myself cosmopolitan. You seem to forget that the early part of my life was spent in the environs of Buenos Aires, and while I was doing my medical training I lived in Madrid. Because I would demand fidelity from my own wife it doesn't mean that I hold the creed of the Dark Ages or that I would be unsympathetic towards her visiting a close relative without me.'

'But you would prefer she didn't?' Merle refused to back down. Cosmopolitan or not, Rico was Latin and male. She didn't need a crystal ball to understand the temperament that dwelt in his lean hard body, the complex character formed by a culture where harsh moral strictures reflected on one's own virtue, for hadn't she already received ample evidence of his intolerance? Only Rico hadn't always been virtuous, had he? she reminded herself. Hadn't he hinted at some affair he had once had with a married woman? She was looking at a convert, and they were notoriously rigid in their views—everyone knew that!

Rico was regarding her closely as if his clear eyes could read her innermost thoughts. 'Let us just say that any feeling of indifference towards her holiday destination would undoubtedly be compensated for by the pleasure of sharing her company,' he replied smoothly. 'Perhaps you judge your stepfather too harshly?'

He was leaning back in his chair now, half turned so that she was the full object of his concentration. One of his bare tanned arms lay languidly along the arm of the chair, fingers lightly cupping its end, the other was bent on the other arm so that one thumb and forefinger rested against his cheek. Only the intensity of his stare belied the casual laziness of his lounging body.

Afterwards she was never sure why she confided in him. Perhaps it had been the effect of the shimmering heat, the headiness of the wine cup or her repeated awareness of his potent charisma that had caught her in its charm so long ago and was now reaching out to entrap her once more. Perhaps it was just because she felt the need to release some of the miserable pent-up memories of her earlier life or simply because she felt the need to justify to her condescending companion the antipathy she felt for the man her mother had married.

'Is it possible to find an excuse for a man who marries a widow with two young daughters and then shows every evidence of hating them?'

'It's even difficult to find a reason, Merlita.' Rico's response was gentle, as if he were aware of the tightly battened emotions that threatened to burst free whenever she thought of the kind of life they had been forced to lead.

'He was jealous because she loved us—I realise that now, but I can't forgive him. He wanted all her attention all the time, resenting our need for her.' She paused as the waiter placed more bread on the table, waiting until he was out of earshot before continuing dully, 'I was five, my sister Barbara eight when she remarried. Too young to understand that whatever we did, however we behaved, we would always be in the wrong...' She stopped speaking, swallowing the lump in her throat.

'Was he cruel to you, Merle?' There was a deep pity in Rico's voice as his hand left the arm of the chair to cover her straining fingers.

'Not physically,' she whispered, remembering the cold silences, the harsh instructions, the icy discipline which had denied both Barbara and herself any contact with friends or amusements outside of school. Even when they had left school and found work, Barbara as a clerk in a local supermarket and she as an assistant in a chain store, their social life had been non-existent.

'I see.' Rico nodded as if he understood all the things she couldn't tell him, reading the truth in the unhappiness that darkened her eyes. 'But you managed to leave home eventually?'

'When I was eighteen, yes. Barbara fell in love with one of the mechanics who serviced the supermarket's fleet of vans. Grant is a super person, not the kind of man to be cowed by anyone, but even he couldn't persuade my stepfather to agree to their getting married.' Merle shivered, reliving the past. 'There was a dreadful row, and I think if it hadn't been for Grant's determination Barbara would have given in and refused to see him again. As it was, he persuaded her to elope with him. It wasn't as if they needed anyone's permission— just that Barbara so wanted a family blessing at the start of a new life.'

'That must have made matters much worse for you and your mother.' With unerring accuracy Rico homed in on what had happened.

'It was awful.' Merle spoke so softly he had to lean towards her to catch her answer. 'Barbara and Grant moved down south to the London suburbs and as soon as they were settled they offered me and Mother a home. Mother refused, but she begged me to go. I didn't want to leave her, but eventually she persuaded me that if she were alone with my stepfather things would improve, that it was seeing us—the fruits of her love for our real

father—that was making him so unreasonable. She felt
that if they were on their own matters would improve.'

'And did they?' Rico prompted gently as she paused.

'I don't know.' Merle shook her head, staring out into
the bright sunlight and seeing nothing but the internal
images of a dark cheerless house in the Scottish country-
side. 'That was five years ago. Barbara and I write to
her regularly and her replies are always cheerful, but we
know it could only worsen matters if we ever went back
there, and Mum won't agree to meet us outside the
house—so...' She left the sentence in mid-air.

There was no need to finish it for Rico to gather how
desperately she prayed for her mother's happiness; her
love and concern were mirrored on her expressive face.

'So perhaps now you understand why my judgement
of my mother's husband is so harsh!' Pride tightened
the line of her jaw as she challenged Rico to question
her reactions.

'Indeed, I now understand many things.' He signalled
for a passing waiter to serve them with coffee, remaining
silent while their cups were filled. 'And it was while you
were living with your sister and her husband that you
met David?'

Merle nodded. She'd been desperate for work. Barbara
and Grant had been living on a council estate near the
factory where Grant had found work. It was a two-
bedroomed house and Barbara had already been
expecting Natalie. With little experience Merle had anticipated difficulty in finding work, so when she had seen
an advertisement for a live-in home help she'd rushed
to apply. That was where she had met David and his wife
Rosemary in their beautiful house in its acres of ground
only two miles away from the industrial settlement where
her sister lived. Two miles—but it could have been in
another world!

'And he was kind and wealthy and he wanted you?'
There was no edge to Rico's voice, just the polite enquiry.

'Yes.' Both David and Rosemary had warmed to her
immediately. The latter had explained that at the age of
thirty-nine and after fifteen years of marriage she was
unexpectedly and delightfully expecting a baby. David,
fifteen years her senior, was also thrilled, but concerned
because of her age.

'It's absurd, my dear,' she had confided with a grin.
'I'm as fit as a fiddle, and after all, it's fashionable now
to wait until you're in your thirties before starting a
family, but David's insisting I give up work and have
help around the house, and I'm not going to argue with
him!'

'So you exchanged your youth and your beauty for
his protection and his patronage.' It was a statement,
not a question. It was also a condemnation that brought
the blood surging to Merle's pale cheeks. He knew
nothing, nothing! How dared he stand in judgement on
her? For a few moments she had been deceived by what
she had misread as his compassion. His pity had been
skin-deep, beneath the surface his condemnation of her
burnt as fiercely as ever!

'I married David because he wanted me to and because I loved and respected him!' It was not entirely a
lie. Pity, after all, was said to be akin to love, and when
Rosemary had suffered a fatal brain haemorrhage six
months after Laurie's birth her heart had overfilled with
pity for the dazed and shocked widower.

Not that marriage had entered either of their heads at
that time. No, it had been two years later that David
had proposed to her—and only then because he knew
he was dying and Laurie would be left destitute. Once
she was the little girl's stepmother no one could chal-

lenge her authority to continue bestowing the love and
care she was already lavishing on her!

It had been no sacrifice. She and Rosemary had
learned together about looking after babies, both as ig-
norant and enthusiastic as each other at the start! Far
from being merely employer and employee they had
become firm friends in their limited time together, each
devoted to Laurie and cognisant of her needs. After the
trauma of Rosemary's unexpected death Merle had
automatically taken over full care for the child, loving
her as if she'd been her own, and David, inconsolable
in his grief, had been only too relieved for her to do
so...

None of which she was about to explain to the man
tossing down his coffee at her side with complete disregard for its heat. She owed him nothing, least of all
the exposure of her soul!

As he replaced the cup in its saucer Rico reached for
her left hand, running his forefinger over the band of
gold that encircled her ring finger.

'Not because he could afford to buy you villas in
Spain?' His mouth stretched in a humourless smile.
'Then I suggest that out of the respect you claim for him
you always remember to keep his ring on your finger.'

After the empathy she had been tricked into believing
they'd shared his remark was like a slap round the face
and it was all Merle could do not to gasp. Abruptly she
removed her hand from his hold, not deigning to answer.
There was a sober truth in his advice. David had entrusted Laurie to her with a blind faith that she would
always do what was best for his daughter. It was a
trusteeship she intended to honour, regardless of the
consequences it might have on her own future!

'Finish your coffee.' Rico's curt nod in the direction
of her cup signified the end of the subject. 'It's time we

were leaving, if you want to try and claim Paraiso tonight.'

'Señora Costain!' Juan Montero advanced across the floor of his pleasant first-floor office in one of Seville's modern blocks to greet them, hand extended, eyes flicking swiftly from Merle to the man who accompanied her.

There was something about his manner—a kind of defensiveness which immediately alerted her. Despite the festering indignation she was still harbouring against him, Merle was suddenly very glad to have Rico at her side.

'May I introduce Señor de Montilla?' Deliberately she didn't define Rico's role, not that she was sure of it herself! But it wouldn't hurt the dapper little lawyer to see she wasn't on her own if he was going to make any difficulties about handing over the deeds of her property. Maybe he would even be fooled by Rico's professional bearing into believing she had brought her own legal counsel with her.

As the two men gravely shook hands Merle subsided in the seat offered to her. 'I've come to collect the deeds of the Villa Paraiso,' she began without preamble as Rico took the seat beside her. 'I understood from the Bennets that they'd be ready for me as soon as I arrived?' she smiled brightly, her heart beginning to increase its beat as Juan Montero's brows drew together in a puzzled frown.'

'You didn't receive my letter, then, *señora*?' he questioned.

'What letter?' Merle leaned forward towards the desk.

'The letter where I explained about the court case.'

'What court case?' The sense of doom she had felt began to increase. 'I've received no letter and I know nothing about any court case. All I'm asking for is the deeds to the property I've bought and paid for!'

'I'm afraid that's not possible any longer, *señora*...' The Spanish solicitor was obviously ill at ease, his accented English thickening a little, his glance darting from her face to linger momentarily on Rico's quietly perceptive features. 'It is a matter of law, you see. Unfortunately the Bennets weren't the original owners—they purchased the property from a speculator. Before he sold it to them he had certain alterations effected by a local tradesman—and unfortunately these were never paid for. For ten years this builder has waited for payment. When he heard the villa was changing hands yet again he took his claim to court....' Heavy shoulders beneath the smart grey suit shrugged philosophically. 'The bad debt was proved and the judge awarded him the villa in compensation. There is nothing to be done.... *lo siento mucho, señora*....'

'But the villa cost me over six million pesetas! This is madness!' There was a pain in Merle's chest and she could actually feel the blood pounding in her ears, as her voice soared out of control. It wasn't possible that she'd lost tens of thousands of pounds of her dead husband's legacy—the legacy she'd vowed to guard and tend for Laurie's future.

The villa had been intended not only as a memorial to David but as an investment as well as a personal haven of holiday enjoyment. Nausea made her swallow violently as her eyes flamed at the discomfited Montero.

'Relax, Merle.' The calmly spoken words bounced meaninglessly off her ears as Rico moved at last to place his arm firmly round her shoulders. 'Whatever has happened, Señor Montero is not to blame.'

Relief was mirrored in the older man's eyes as he launched into a rapid exposition in his native tongue, gesticulating with his hands, apparently soliciting Rico's understanding. Still dazed, Merle allowed the fast exchange of Spanish to continue without interruption. Thank goodness Rico had been with her! Clearly there had been some absurd misunderstanding. She would raise the amount required to pay off the debt and her villa would be returned to her. She breathed deeply, feeling her nerves begin to steady. She'd been stupid to panic.

'Entiendo, entiendo....' Rico smiled pleasantly, accepting a slip of paper from the other man, as their conversation appeared to reach a satisfactory conclusion. 'Gracias, señor.'

Following Rico's example, Merle found herself shaking hands with the lawyer, before allowing herself to be led from the office and escorted outside into the heat of the street.

'But this is monstrous! If that's the law then it should be changed!' Outside on the pavement she blazed her protest into Rico's set face.

'I agree.' His calm acceptance of her scorn did nothing to placate her, as memories rushed back to alert her.

'You knew, didn't you?' she accused breathlessly. 'Yesterday, when I told you what had happened . . . you knew!'

'I suspected the possibility,' he admitted gravely. 'It's not the first time it's happened, and all the signs were there.'

'And you didn't even warn me!' She didn't stop to consider that he might have done her a favour by letting her have a night's sleep devoid of anxiety as her fury gathered force. 'I suppose you're glad! You never really wanted me here, did you? What was it you called me— a coqueta? I guess you're glad I've lost everything, that I won't be around to lower the tone of the place . . .' Her voice shook with anger. 'What a sadistic pleasure you

must have been enjoying all this time at my expense!'
Taking a deep breath, she fought to gain control of her
emotions. Unless she was careful she was going to burst
into tears of frustration, and that would never do!

Raising one dark eyebrow in a gesture she was beginning to recognise, Rico waited patiently for her to
calm down with an attitude of laboured courtesy that
made her blood run cold. How he must detest her! The
dreadful thing was, she *needed* his advice. The shock of
events had annihilated her usual reserves of mental
strength. She felt stunned, unable to make any kind of
rational decision as to what her next move must be.

'What—what do I do now?' she whispered, drained
of every vestige of pride, as she raised beseeching eyes
to his austere countenance.

'There is obviously only one thing you can do.' Rico
paused meaningfully. 'You must get in touch with your
husband, wherever he is, without delay, and let him know
what has occurred. The final responsibility, after all, is
surely his.'

This was it, then. The final crunch. No longer was
she going to be able to protect herself with the power of
another man's presence in her life—however distant. 'I—
I can't.' Her reply was little more than a murmur, as her
eyes closed in spontaneous pain. 'David and I are no
longer—together.'

'You're divorced!' Rico's voice was sharp with
amazement. 'No, no, I don't believe that! There has not
been sufficient time for divorce, even under your liberal
laws. Legally separated, then? Your wealthy husband has
grown tired of your little games, hmm?' He took her by
the shoulders, hauling her so close to his own body that
she could feel the warmth of his flesh radiating through
the flimsy covering of her dress. 'Have I guessed right,
Merle? You bought the villa with the settlement he made

on you, and now you've lost everything? The egg from
the golden goose has been snatched from your predatory little hands, never to be regained?'

'Stop it!' Merle had had enough. On top of the shock
she had just received Rico's determination to attribute
to her the lowest possible motives was more than she
could bear. 'How dare you judge my reasons for marrying David or criticise our relationship?' Tears blinding
her eyes, she tried to detach herself from his predatory
hold, digging her nails into the hard strength of his upper
arms in an effort to obtain her release.

'*Basta!* Enough!' Her struggles were useless as he ignored the pain she was inflicting on the taut muscles at
the mercy of her fingertips, and the musky exciting scent
of his displeasure invaded her heightened senses. Suddenly she felt energy draining from her as she half col-
lapsed against his vibrant strength, her hands
relinquishing their attack to clutch at his imprisoning
arms to save herself from falling.

'I demand an answer.' Rico's voice was low and intense, close to her ear. 'This is no business for a woman.
If your ex-husband's involved in this transaction he
should be here with you now! So you're going to tell me
exactly where he is at this moment!'

He wasn't going to let her go, allow her to merge into
the colourful crowds, as she desired, and suddenly it
didn't matter what she told him. She'd been financially
raped with the connivance of the law. She was wounded,
angry and totally vulnerable, excruciatingly aware that
she could no longer shelter beneath the cover of her
mythical marriage.

Flinging back her head, she said clearly, 'My husband
is dead. He died six months ago.' When she actually
spoke the words she felt relief, even a moment of triumph
as the blank shock wiped Rico's expression clear.

Time seemed to stand still as her words died to silence and neither of them moved a muscle. It was Rico who broke the frozen tableau, taking her cold hand in his own.

'Come, this is no place to discuss our next move. We cannot stay here in the street forever gazing into each other's eyes with such intensity or we will be suspected of having a lovers' quarrel!'

He was right. Latin curiosity was already making them the centre of attraction—besides, like it as little as she did, Rico remained her only link with sanity! As if in a dream Merle allowed herself to be led silently through the crowded streets back to the place where the car had been parked.

It was only when they were once more on the road out of Seville that Rico broke the silence between them.

'Your husband's death was sudden?' His eyes on the road, he presented his cool profile to her quick glance.

'Not really. He'd been ill for some time.' She wasn't going to tell him her shock of learning that David had Hodgkin's Disease or her dismay when it was clear that unlike the vast majority of cases which were curable David's was diagnosed as terminal. She wouldn't divulge how much greater her distress had been than David's, the latter having accepted the news with a resignation that had much to do with his adamantine faith that he would be reunited with his beloved wife, only the thought of leaving alone the little girl who had been the fruit of their love torturing him.

She sighed reminiscently. It had been an easy decision for her to make a marriage of convenience to ensure that Laurie's young life would have some degree of continuity. She would have done it, whatever David's circumstances had been, out of love for the child and her affection for Rosemary, but for his part David had been quick to point out that he wouldn't have considered such a possibility unless he'd known she would be comfortably off after his death, assured of an income not only from his investments but by the regular royalties she would receive from his publishers. As he was a compiler of scientific textbooks which were sold to schools and universities all over the world, David's income from this source had been as healthy as any popular fiction writer's—probably more healthy than most!

It had been Barbara who had been more impressed with this aspect of the future when Merle had confided her intentions, pointing out that with a dependent child her sister's chances of finding future happiness for herself would be much improved if she had a private income.

'There aren't many men who can afford to take on another man's child, even if emotionally they're prepared to do so,' she had told Merle soberly. 'Especially when they find out that you're not Laurie's real mother. Are you quite sure you know what you're doing?'

'Quite sure.' Merle had had no doubts. 'Laurie needs me. As far as marriage is concerned I've never even thought about it.' She'd laughed. 'Perhaps I'm a natural spinster!'

'Or perhaps you've never been in love.'

Her sister's clear voice echoed in her memory. Of course Barbie knew she'd never been in love. Never even had a boyfriend. Even seeing Barbie and Grant so happy in each other's company and the warmth between David and Rosemary so evident, Merle had never imagined herself falling in love. Her contact with the opposite sex had been so limited she supposed she was just unawakened.

She must try to keep her problems in perspective. Even if she had lost a large sum of money she wasn't by any standards broke. It was just that she felt so unworthy of the trust David had invested in her.

Beside her Rico sat silent, concentrating on driving, and she was glad that he wasn't going to pursue the state of David's health at their last meeting. The illness had been in a period of remission when her husband had expressed a wish to return for the last time to the Costa de la Luz, and she had willingly agreed. For those few weeks in the sun he had appeared contented with no signs of distress except extreme tiredness. On their return his condition had deteriorated rapidly and fatally. Watching the passing landscape, Merle decided that Rico had formed his own opinion once more, and whatever it was, it would almost certainly be to her own detriment.

CHAPTER FIVE

ARRIVING at the Villa Jazmin, Merle allowed Rico to usher her into the pleasant living-room, sinking wearily on to one of the couches. His silence during the drive had given her plenty of time to appraise her situation, and, although she still couldn't come to terms with it, she had formed a plan of action.

'I hate to trouble you further,' she told him stiffly as he stood looking down at her, 'but I'd be very grateful if you could drive me to one of the hotels on the beach. I think the best thing I can do is get a room somewhere while I try to arrange a flight back to England.'

'Running away?' he asked smoothly.

'Cutting my losses.' Her chin came up defiantly at his tone. 'Since I've been assured on such good authority that I can't fight the law, there's no point in my staying here, is there?'

'Probably not,' Rico agreed calmly, standing a few feet in front of her and gazing down at her, 'but, on the other hand, you should explore all avenues before surrendering. For instance, I obtained from Montero the name and address of the man who now owns the Villa Paraiso.' He withdrew from his pocket the slip of paper she had seen him place there in Montero's office. 'His name is Sanchez and he lives on the outskirts of Seville. I understand he's already put the villa back on the market, but he might be amenable to reason.'

'Appeal to his sense of chivalry, you mean?' Her eyes flashed scornfully. 'I thought you said his name was Sanchez, not Quixote!'

A glimmer in Rico's dark eyes appreciated her acidity. 'Sometimes calm talk can prevail over anger. Señor Sanchez has waited ten years for repayment, he has a right to be angry. However, he may not be a man of great greed. Having been compensated more than justly he may be open to reason.' There was a gleam behind his dark eyes she couldn't put a name to. 'We Andalusians are quickly aroused to passion, but we are generous too if our sensibilities are honoured!'

'You think I should approach him personally?' she asked doubtfully, willing to clutch at any straw, however slender.

'If all else fails that might be the solution.' Rico appraised her upturned face with deep interest. 'Depending on the kind of man Sanchez is and the type of price you are prepared to pay, it might be possible to come to an agreement.'

He couldn't mean——? Merle felt the blood rise from her neck to scald to her forehead, but before she could put her thoughts into words he was continuing unhurriedly, 'The best thing to do is to hire a local lawyer with real-estate experience and have him act as an intermediary between yourself and Sanchez or Sanchez's own legal representative. That way you will learn exactly what you're up against and determine if there is any way to mitigate your loss.'

'Is it really worth it?' Professional help never came cheap, and every penny she spent was robbing Laurie.

'I think so,' Rico nodded firmly. 'Not all faith in human nature is misplaced. A compromise solution might still be possible.' His broad shoulders moved lazily beneath their covering. 'The payment of the outstanding debt plus accrued interest charges, for instance. That would be acceptable to you, yes?'

'Yes! Yes, of course!' It seemed such a vain hope, but one she couldn't afford to turn her back on.

'Good! I know just the very man to act on your behalf. He manages all the real-estate deals my brother Armando makes. He's trustworthy and ultra-efficient. If anyone can find a means of negotiation Fidelio Diaz can!'

Merle felt as if her brain were overflowing like some malfunctioning computer: the only stable thing in her life appearing to be the tall, powerful figure of the man staring down at her awaiting her response. Why would he want to help her? Had his discovery of her widowhood softened his attitude towards her? Was it pure altruism born from compassion—or was there some ulterior motive in this sudden offer of assistance? Clearly if David had been alive she would have been offered no such advice!

Briefly she closed her eyes, envisaging the Villa Paraiso—her and Laurie's villa—bought from the savings David had accrued and entrusted to her. Of course she had no option. She must take every possible step open to her, even though it meant putting herself under obligation to a man who had made no attempt to conceal his contempt for her.

'Then I agree we should try, if Señor Diaz is prepared to handle the problem,' she decided firmly, adding softly, 'And thank you for suggesting it.'

'Oh, he'll accept it.' Rico's smile was only slightly malicious. 'When he knows it's Montilla business!'

'But it's not!' Merle protested as he sat down nonchalantly on the arm of the couch where she rested.

'You're my guest—therefore it's my business.' He waved a dismissive hand.

'But I'm not going to be your guest any longer,' Merle said quickly. 'That's why I asked you to take me to a hotel. I can't possibly stay here another night—you must realise that.'

'Why?' The blank question forced her frankness.

'Because yesterday was different. It was too late to get a taxi and—and...' She paused, her eyes pleading him to understand but not comment on what he must know were her reservations.

She was to be disappointed. 'Because last night I thought you were married and tonight I know that to be untrue?'

'Something like that.' Merle couldn't meet the cool assessment of his brilliant eyes, glancing away as his hand rose to take her chin, but there was to be no gentle acceptance of her scruples.

'And because I told you that I once desired you, and even now—although that adolescent yearning has evaporated like the morning dew in midsummer—you must be aware that I am still enchanted by your false projection of unworldliness and your undeniable physical beauty?'

Her face was swung gently but firmly so her eyes could meet his level gaze, as she gasped at his frankness. His words affected her even more than the feel of his hand on her skin. To hear herself described as beautiful in a voice of such deep enthralling timbre was as erotic as a caress, although it had been no compliment.

'You're afraid to stay under my roof because you think I still desire you enough to creep into your room in the middle of the night and claim the treasure you promised me now I know you have no male protector? Is that your reason, Merlita?'

'I only know you regard me as mercenary and immoral.' Merle forced herself to speak calmly with a supreme effort, unable to deny her awareness of his desire for her, a desire coupled with disgust both for herself and himself for harbouring it. The tension between them was like static electricity. Even now, Rico's fingers on her chin were sending thrills of feeling down her nervous system, unwelcome and unsettling, like nothing she had ever experienced before.

He gave a short laugh, his fingers moving from her chin to stroke her cheek, while she sat transfixed. 'My feelings may be ambivalent where you are concerned, but I would never transgress the rules of hospitality. You are as safe here as you would be in a nunnery, I promise you—if that is what you want.'

If it was what she wanted! How dared he even suggest anything different?

'There's no lock on my door,' she said crisply. 'If I did accept your offer I would require your word that you wouldn't come in without knocking first.'

Remembering how he must have seen her spread out on the bed when he had taken her key earlier, Merle felt the colour rise to her cheeks. How wanton she must have looked, her breasts bare, her hair tumbled against the white pillow! She saw the frown crease his brow as he observed the change in her complexion.

'You're suggesting that you didn't hear my knock this morning and invite me in?' He regarded her coldly. 'Your memory appears unusually short.'

Merle met his stony gaze unflinchingly. 'I'm referring to earlier on when you took the key of the Villa Paraiso from my purse while I was still asleep.'

'You misjudge me.' Rico considered her outraged expression thoughtfully, his mouth drawn into a grim line. 'Although from your blushes I almost wish I had committed such an indelicate intrusion. I obviously missed a delightful sight!' The glitter behind his dark eyes could have been amusement or anger as he continued. 'The truth is, you left your jacket downstairs last night and when I went to hang it up in the lobby for you the key fell out of the pocket. To borrow it was a liberty I felt justified in taking in your own interests.'

'Oh!' Both hands rose to her burning cheeks, as she remembered thrusting the key in her pocket after having made her decision to go to the Villa Jazmin. Relief and remorse flooded through her. 'I'm sorry, Rico.' In her embarrassment she couldn't meet his haughty appraisal, staring down at her own hands as she made her apology.

'Gracias.' He rose to his feet, extending a hand to her so that she too rose to stand facing him. 'There's one thing you should know about me, Merle. I'm no saint and I've crossed thresholds that many would condemn me for—but never uninvited. Never! And I'm not so insensitive as not to realise that there is a great difference between a married woman seeking extra-marital amusement and a widow who has to replan her future on a long-term basis.' Blithely he ignored her hiss of indrawn breath as he continued without a pause, 'So, tonight you stay here. We will spend a pleasant evening listening to music and taking refreshment, enjoy an early night in our separate rooms and face tomorrow and its problems when it comes.'

Merle was really too tired to argue, and there was a remarkable degree of comfort in having Rico concern himself so deeply with her affairs, whatever his motives. Her sense of isolation had been banished. Even if nothing came of it she would have the satisfaction of knowing her lack of language had not prejudiced her chances of beating the system.

He was still watching her intently and she realised he was waiting for her agreement. Taking a deep breath, she made her mind up, deciding that despite his tendency to place himself next to God when it came to judging his fellow human beings—perhaps even because of it—Rico de Montilla was very much a man of his word.

'Then I gratefully accept your invitation.'

'Good!'

Then before she realised his intention he dipped his dark head and kissed her briefly but firmly on her mouth.

'Just remember not to issue any of your own, won't you?'

Merle slept badly that night, her slumber beset by dreams in which she relived the stress of the previous months when she'd been forced to carry on her domestic duties as if nothing were wrong both for David's and Laurie's sakes.

Barbie had been wonderful, her original qualms stilled when she had seen how devoted the little girl and her sister were. It hadn't only been moral support her older sister had offered either, Merle accorded the next morning, pulling a face at her image in the bathroom mirror as she saw the heavy shadows beneath her eyes. Barbie and Grant had kept an open house for both herself and Laurie, often having the latter to stay with them so that Merle could spend hours at a time at David's bedside during the final few days.

It had been a great comfort knowing that Laurie enjoyed staying with her auntie Barbie and playing with Natalie. It was one of the reasons Merle had reluctantly left her behind in England while she made a preliminary inspection of the villa, rather than submit her to an uncertain routine. She missed her dreadfully already, but in the circumstances it was just as well! Today she'd phone England to check that everything was all right and to break the bad news to her sister.

Sighing, she applied a light covering of pink lipstick to her mouth in order to add a little colour to her face, trying to lessen the effect of lack of sleep. If she were honest it wasn't only the dreams that had disturbed her. It had been several hours before she had even lost consciousness, lying there with her mind full of Rico. Dear heavens, how she hated to be in his debt when he so obviously despised her! But what reasonable alternative had she had? She shuddered, recalling the pressure of his mouth against her own as he'd warned her not to issue any invitations.

Did she really think she was so promiscuous and lacking in pride that she would offer herself to him when he had attacked her so scathingly? And that remark about promising him treasure! She supposed she should have denied it at the time, but what was the point? In his eyes she was the original scarlet woman... And as for re-planning her future on a long-term basis...the only plan she had in mind was that of providing Laurie with love and security...

Dressing herself in pale lilac trousers topped with a darker mauve sleeveless shirt knotted at the waist, she admitted grimly to herself that in Rico's eyes her virtue was certainly suspect! An opinion that made his charity even more difficult to bear.

For a moment last night her hand had tensed, the muscles of her arm knotting as she had fought the impulse to smack his autocratic face as he had stepped back from embracing her. To have done so would have forfeited his help, logic had argued with her, and she needed that help if she was to do the best for Laurie.

She sighed. If she were honest with herself, there'd been more to it than that. On a purely physical level Rico's nearness to her, the caress of his hard silky mouth, the touch of his hands on her arms had not been unpleasant. Confusing, disturbing, insulting—yes, but although she had felt the contempt in his dismissal she had been aware of an underlying tug of attraction, the same magnetism that had drawn her to him in the first place when she had been so dazed with the pressure of her unhappiness she had responded automatically to his warmth and tenderness.

Returning to the bed, she smoothed the covers back into place. What warmth and tenderness, she asked herself bitterly, and how long would Rico expect her to stay? Another day perhaps, while he contacted his brother's lawyer? More than that would be an impossible imposition, she determined fiercely. Rico de Montilla wasn't the only one around with unmitigated pride. She had her fair share too, and it wouldn't allow her to accept his hospitality a day longer than necessary.

Firmly she quashed the idle thought that she could explain to her censorious host about the terms of her marriage. In the first place it was none of his business. In the second place it would be ridiculous to expect him to find the circumstances mitigating. He was too endowed with that Latin pride that saw marriage, any kind of marriage, as sacred and binding.

Angrily Merle thumped one of the pillows. For that matter, she shared the same belief—it had been David who had insisted that she was perfectly free to live her own kind of life, form her own attachments even while she was still nominally his wife. In fact he had positively encouraged her to do so, which was why she had felt no guilt in seeking Rico out each afternoon. The latter had been a friend, a like spirit—or that was what, in her innocence, she had imagined at the time!

So, she decided, it was far better to keep silent, maintaining the uneasy peace that existed between them. She was being childish and unrealistic in wanting to regain his approbation. All that mattered now was trying to retrieve something from the fiasco into which she'd plunged herself.

Casually dressed in pale grey trousers and a white open-necked shirt, Rico was in the living-room, a cup of coffee in his hand.

'*Buenos días,*' he greeted her formally, rising lazily to his full height. 'To avoid any misunderstanding I waited for you to come down before offering you breakfast.'

Merle's cheeks heated under the light flick of his eyes as she ignored his sarcasm.

'Good morning,' she returned stiffly, as he bent to the elegant coffee-table before the couch and filled a waiting cup, offering it to her.

'Thank you.' Seating herself opposite him, perching on the edge of the couch, she wondered why the sight of him so relaxed and in command filled her with such mixed feelings of fierce antagonism and equally vivid attraction, as she waved away his offer of croissants. 'Thank you, I'm not hungry this morning.'

'A bad night?' His sympathy was accompanied by a close scrutiny of her wan face. 'I'm afraid you suffered a very traumatic experience yesterday, and staying here alone with me can hardly have added to your peace of mind.'

Meeting his ironic expression, Merle lifted a casual shoulder. 'I worried about the villa, yes, of course I did, but as far as you were concerned I accepted your undertaking at face-value.' It was true. It had never occurred to her that he would break his word.

'I'm flattered.' His coolly cynical gaze lingered on her face. 'Nevertheless, your original misgivings were justified. It isn't suitable for you and me to be living under the same roof without a chaperon, so I have arranged alternative accommodation for you as you originally requested.'

'Oh, but that's marvellous!' Merle smiled her relief, delighted that she was going to be released from the strange tension of the atmosphere surrounding her. 'I was afraid all the hotels might be fully booked. Which one is it, and for how long have you booked a room?'

'It's an open-ended reservation.' Rico took a casual sip of his coffee. 'These things can't be hurried.'

His cool, level gaze was somehow unnerving, causing the small pulse at the base of her throat to hammer in sudden apprehension. 'But I have to get home to Laurie——'

'Or arrange for her to come out here to you?'

'Well, that was the original plan. Once the villa was cleaned up and sufficiently furnished Grant and Barbie were coming over with Natalie and Laurie and all four of them were going to stay.'

'So you must have allowed yourself a week to get things in order?'

'Yes, I did—but in the circumstances...'

'In the circumstances you still have a few days left. You can phone your sister and let her know what's happening. If at the end of the week...' Rico paused, shrugging his shoulders, his action needing no explanation.

It was patently clear that if nothing had been resolved in seven days she would never set eyes on the Villa Paraiso again unless she was prepared to repurchase it. Desire it as she did, she would never be able to justify putting good money after bad.

'I guess you're right,' she sighed with resignation. 'I'm grateful for your finding me a hotel. Where is it?'

Watching the corners of his mouth deepen into what could only be a suppressed smile, and the sudden challenging sparkle at the back of his dark eyes, Merle was filled with instant foreboding.

'As you so rightly surmised, all the hotels along the coast are fully booked. The place where you'll be staying is called the Cortijo del Rey—and it's not a hotel. It's my brother's farm,' Rico announced serenely.

'Oh, but I can't!' Horrified, Merle sprang to her feet. 'How could you suggest a thing? You can't inflict a stranger's company on them!'

'Hardly a stranger, surely?' he baited her softly. 'Have you forgotten all the good moments we shared last year?'

It was a question Merle refused to answer. She might not have forgotten them, but Rico's present attitude had besmirched their memory. How she wished she could put their lingering sweetness out of her mind forever!

'I'm sorry.' She shook her head, full of determination. 'For one thing, I've only brought casual clothes with me, I should feel out of place and miserable. I'd—I'd rather stay here.'

Who would have thought she would ever make such an admission? And the low laugh which greeted it brought a flood of colour to her face.

'You may have no need to preserve your good name, but for me it's imperative.' Rico's dark eyes mocked her embarrassment and for a moment she thought he must be joking. 'It's perfectly true.' He'd caught her wide-eyed disbelief and proceeded to demolish it. 'The clinic which employs me is supported by many Christian charities. In return for their generosity they expect the highest level of ethics to be demonstrated by their practitioners—both professional and moral. To have you stay for two nights in an emergency——' he made a careless gesture with one beautiful long-fingered hand '—that would be acceptable. But to keep you under my roof for a week—ah——' the dark head shook chidingly '—that would make the idle tongues gossip—and bring me into certain confrontation with my employers' benefactors.'

'You mean they would demand you were dismissed?' she asked incredulously.

'Or married, to regularise the situation.' A cynical sparkle brought a golden gleam to his dark regard. 'Take your choice.' His eyes rested on her, alive with cool speculation, indolently awaiting her reaction.

He'd deliberately set out to infuriate her, and she wasn't going to rise to his bait. A disdainful shrug was intended to demonstrate her indifference.

'A good doctor can always find work. You'd soon be re-employed.'

'But I enjoy the job I have and intend to keep it, or at least,' Rico amended smoothly, 'to sacrifice it for far greater rewards than your continued presence here.' He rose to stand over her. 'Neither, like you, do I find the alternative appealing, so I'm afraid if the matter of your property is to be contended you'll have to do as I've arranged . . . and stay at the *cortijo*.'

An angry tautness held Merle immobile as she felt her tenuous grasp on events slipping away. It was too much of an imposition on people she didn't know, yet the only real alternative was to get a flight back to England as soon as possible and forsake even this last forlorn hope of regaining Paraiso.

'Don't be foolhardy, Merle.' Unexpectedly Rico's hand came to rest on her shoulder. 'To be honest, you'd be doing my sister-in-law a great favour. My brother Armando is in Madrid on business at the moment, and Pavane would dearly love company. Of course, she's got the children and the household staff, but it's not the same as having a fellow-countrywoman to talk to, is it? This morning when I phoned her she was absolutely thrilled with the idea and looking forward to hearing all the news from England.'

'Your brother's wife is English?' Startled, Merle wasn't aware how her expression lightened with interest and pleasure.

'Indeed yes. I've already explained your predicament to her, and she'll be a staunch ally on your behalf, I can assure you. In fact, at my request she's already alerted Señor Diaz of the problem and is trying to arrange a meeting between the three of us at the *cortijo* tomorrow.'

'But—but I hadn't accepted her invitation...'

'She assumed you would, since I suggested it.' Rico paused slightly before adding, 'I explained how I met you—and your family—last year and your present circumstances. A white lie, I believe you call it? Preferable, I'm sure you will agree, to the absolute truth.'

'Which is?' Shock mingled with indignant anger as Merle stared at Rico's grim face, daring him to put his reservations into words.

'That last year I was crazy enough to become attracted to you, only to discover that you were a married woman looking for a fling. And that now the only thing that makes me act on your behalf is compassion for the little girl who has lost a father and whose mother is incapable of managing the estate her misguided husband left to her.'

So that was his motive. A form of reparation to the child he had seen so briefly and after whose mother he had fleetingly lusted. Yes, that was the word, Merle thought bitterly. All Rico had felt for her that brief summer had been the natural desire of a young and virile man for what he had assumed to be an available female. While she...she in her naïveté had believed his interest had been rooted in something far less physical. Biting her lip, too weary to defend herself, she looked away.

'So you'll come? Good!' Rico took her silence as tacit agreement, removing his hand from her shoulder with every sign of triumph written on his imposing face. 'We're expected for lunch, so we can leave as soon as you've finished breakfast. It won't take me long to pack.' He moved towards the staircase as the impact of his words struck her.

'You mean you'll be staying at the *cortijo* too? But I thought...'

'That I'd stay here?' He regarded her as if she were abnormally simple. 'When Fidelio Diaz is going to call at the *cortijo* that would seem a very unrealistic situation, unless you feel confident enough to brief him yourself?'

'I thought you just wanted to get rid of me,' Merle mumbled, letting her eyes drop from his derisive gaze. 'You could have briefed him by phone—and besides, what about your work?'

'I've a few days to spare,' came the lazy answer. 'The clinic is undergoing renovation work and only emergency cases are being admitted. If I'm needed I'll make sure I can be contacted.'

Merle glanced back at him uncertainly, trying to assimilate the import of this new development. 'It's very good of you to put yourself out on my behalf like this. It makes me feel very guilty.'

'*Verdad?*' A cynical sparkle illuminated his charismatic eyes. 'Then I feel myself well rewarded. Guilt, Merle? That must be a very strange emotion for you to experience. Savour it while it lasts. I doubt it will often be repeated!'

CHAPTER SIX

As a Parthian shot it was unanswerable. All Merle could do was grit her teeth in frustration as she watched Rico's lean powerful frame move purposefully towards the stairs while she nursed the sudden ache in her heart his cruel condemnation had evoked. A year of trauma and tragedy had passed from which she had emerged a stronger more positive person. How was it then that Rico de Montilla still had the power to incite a perverse excitement in her despite the lash of his sarcasm?

It was a question she didn't want to think about, let alone answer. Resolutely she poured herself another cup of coffee from the percolater. The only reason she had even considered his invitation had been for Laurie. If it hadn't been for David's enchanting daughter and the obligation she felt towards her, she'd be on her way home now rather than share a roof with this dominating Spaniard for even one more night!

Despite her strong reservations about the wisdom of her decision, the first sight of the Cortijo del Rey caused Merle to cry out in delight, when they arrived a few hours later.

'It's beautiful!' she exclaimed.

Rico nodded his agreement. 'Mainly because of the work Armando's put into it these past twenty years. When he came here from Argentina on our father's death, I understand it was badly dilapidated. He's restored it from an old crumbling ruin into something like its former glory, modernising it without spoiling its intrinsic beauty.'

Parking his car outside the entrance gates, he continued idly, 'Legend has it that one of the caliphs of Cordoba had it specially built so he could entertain his favourite mistress here. Of course, being Muslim, he had wives and probably a harem as well, but this particular lady was of a noble Spanish family. It seems he was so infatuated with her that he would have given her anything she wanted, but she refused to join his harem. In the event he gave her a son and this farm. The story goes that he would have taken the child and recognised him as his son, but the lady was adamantly opposed to it, so the boy remained with her and took her name.'

'Montilla, you mean?' Merle was fascinated.

'Montilla y Cabra, to be precise.' Rico alighted from the car with swift grace to open the passenger door for her. 'Yes, it seems I can claim an Arab prince among my forebears.' A firm hand supported her elbow as Merle stepped from the car into the blazing sunshine, breathing in the air perfumed with herbs and flowers, closing her eyes in delight as she savoured the warm breeze on her skin.

How easy it was to imagine Rico as a descendant of some Moorish princeling! Dress him in Arab robes, cover his crisp dark hair with a flowing headdress banded with the traditional *'iqal*, boot and spur him and mount him on an Arab stallion and he'd be a match for Saladin himself!

Unpredictably a heady feeling of anticipation thrummed through her nervous system. Rico would not lightly abandon any cause he took up. If anyone could retrieve the Villa Paraiso for her it would be he!

It was with a much lighter heart that she allowed herself to be guided towards the imposing entrance of the *cortijo*, only to see a flutter of colour in the open doorway as a young woman emerged carrying a blonde-haired little girl in her arms and followed by a dark-haired boy a few years older.

'Rico and Merle!' The smile on her exquisitely pretty face was natural and welcoming. 'I'm delighted you could both come—though I wish the circumstances had been happier!' She cast a sympathetic glance towards Merle. 'Both Armando and Rico know how I feel about some of the laws in this part of the world, and, although they tell me that British justice isn't perfect either, I know that in this case they'll both agree it's appalling you should be made to suffer.' She smiled down at the toddler in her arms. 'The children have been so excited ever since they heard you were coming. This is Elena, she's just two, and this——' she reached down to the solemn-eyed little boy at her side '—this is my son, Nacio.'

'How do you do?' Nacio greeted her solemnly in excellent English, extending a small hand.

Smiling, Merle shook it, replying formally, 'How do you do?'

In the next second the solemnity had disappeared completely as Rico stepped forward and lifted the child up in his arms. 'And how about a welcome for your *tío* Rico?' he demanded.

'Put me down!' Nacio squealed happily. 'I'm not a baby any more. I'm five!'

'My, my, how time flies!' Rico pressed his hard cheek against the boy's soft face before flinging him upwards so the child sat astride his shoulders, falling into step beside Merle as their hostess led them into the house.

Pavane was absolutely lovely, Merle accorded admiringly to herself with the simple generosity of one woman acknowledging another's beauty. Probably no more than half a dozen years older than herself,

Armando's wife had the slim but curvaceous figure of a teenager. Soft short blonde hair curled appealingly round a face in which the eyes were the dominant feature, only just marginally more remarkable than the short classic nose and the soft full mouth with its ready smile.

How like her her daughter was, and how different the son. Nacio obviously resembled his father, which meant Armando and Rico must share the same dark handsomeness. His face relaxed, head turned towards the child on his shoulders, strong mouth curved as he teased him in his native tongue, Rico had fleetingly become the person she had met on the beach. The sensitive, humorous man she had believed could be her friend. But her emotions had been blunted by pain, her judgement warped by inexperience, she thought sadly.

Banishing the unwelcome memories from her mind, she followed her hostess into the *cortijo* and up the wide staircase, along a corridor until they reached a heavy wooden door.

'This the room I've prepared for you.' Pavane flicked a quick gaze round as if checking that everything was in order. 'The bathroom's through there,' she indicated a closed door on the left-hand wall, 'and, as you can see, through the archway there's a sitting-room. Pedro will have your case up here in just a few minutes. When you're ready perhaps you'll join us outside on the terrace—I'm sure you're gasping for some refreshment after that drive.'

'Yes, thank you.' Merle returned the other girl's smile, sinking down on the comfortable double bed as the door closed gently behind her hostess. It was the kind of accommodation she imagined one would find in luxury hotels. The room was vast, bisected by an arched opening through which she could see a low coffee-table, two armchairs and an emerald-green velvet chaise-longue.

Shaking her head in bemusement, she absorbed the plain white walls, their bareness relieved by framed prints, the polished wood floor with its soft blue rugs, the exquisite bedroom suite hand-turned in the natural olivewood of the region. Her eyes lingered on the bedside table, the small vase of carnations, the English magazines, a small pile of paperbacks... With a sigh she rose to her feet, making for the window, drawing back the heavy sun-resisting curtains, delighted to find that behind slatted blinds a large double-glazed area included a sliding door which led on to a wrought-iron balcony, from which she could overlook the terraced area and the large expanse of land which formed part of the Montilla estate.

From below came the sound of voices speaking Spanish. It was easy to recognise Pavane's light voice, her tone quick and amused as she responded to the deeper, more vibrant timbre of her brother-in-law. It wasn't necessary to understand what they were saying to be aware of the warmth and friendship that underlined every word.

Feeling as if she were eavesdropping, Merle stepped back into the room, at the same time as a knock on the door heralded the arrival of her suitcase. Since she had travelled lightly, it took her little time to unpack her belongings, smiling wryly to herself as she admitted they were hardly the wardrobe she would have packed if she'd had any idea she might have ended up in such stylish surroundings.

It was over a delicious lunch of gazpacho, followed by grilled lamb cutlets in orange sauce with savoury rice, that Merle felt some of her earlier tension draining away as she found an instant rapport with Rico's sister-in-law.

'You'll have to bring me up to date with what's happening in England,' Pavane smiled across the table at

her. 'As a matter of fact my sister's over there at the
moment with her husband and young son. Rodrigo had
to go over there to a vintners' conference and it was the
ideal opportunity for Melody to revisit some of our old
haunts.'

'Your sister's married to a Spaniard too?' Merle
couldn't keep the surprise from her voice.

'Why so shocked, Merle?' It was Rico whose lazy voice
answered her. 'Surely you've discovered by now that we
hot-blooded Andalusians have a penchant for cold-
blooded Anglo-Saxons? Some say it's the attraction of
opposites, others that deep into the Andalusian nature
is built a masochistic streak that makes us seek out that
which has the power to destroy us.'

'Oh...' For a moment Merle was lost for words as
Rico calmly reached for his wine glass and drained the
last few drops. 'I hope you don't include your sister-in-
law in that racial castigation?' Her eyes regarded his dark
face, the ironic expression, refusing to quail before him.

'Of course not,' he denied easily, flashing a smile of
undeniable sweetness towards Pavane who was regarding him with a slight frown marring the smooth expanse of her forehead. 'Pavane knows I'm one of her
greatest admirers.'

'You must forgive him.' Pavane shot a conspiratorial
glance towards Merle. 'Rico's idiomatic English is
generally excellent, but I imagine he means "cool-
blooded" rather than "cold-blooded".'

'Do I?' he asked. Merle flushed as his contemplative
gaze raked her face. 'Is there a difference, then?'

It was Pavane who answered, with a light laugh.

'I take it you were referring to calmness and composure. "Cold-blooded" means barbaric, ruthless, stony-
hearted... It's not the same thing at all.'

'Then I apologise, of course.' His voice was as expressionless as his face as he dipped his dark head in assumed contrition.

Frustrated by his cool arrogance, Merle felt an untypical anger uncurl inside her. Was it his intention to bait her at every opportunity under the guise of being pleasant? If so, she'd have to learn to combat his sly digs or her stay at the *cortijo* would be untenable.

'But I didn't take your remarks personally.' The smile she conjured up was a masterpiece of sweetness. 'My genes are more Gaelic than Anglo-Saxon, and the former aren't noted either for their coolness or their coldness.' She paused slightly, aware that her hostess was regarding her thoughtfully, and glad that the children were taking their lunch in the nursery and not a part of this delicate emotional fencing, then added softly, 'Particularly when it comes to a fight.'

'That's excellent news!' The other girl neatly bridged the developing tension. 'Because I'm afraid you're in for a hard one as far as trying to gain repossession of your villa is concerned.' She cast a sympathetic look at Merle, waiting until the maid who had served the meal had departed with the empty plates. 'Señor Diaz is coming over here tomorrow morning, but, to be honest, he holds out little hope. The only possibility is that he and the present owner's lawyer can prevail on Sanchez to exercise compassion on your behalf and agree to a compromise.'

'Perhaps I was silly to allow Rico to persuade me to come here. It's obviously a lost cause...' Merle swallowed the sudden lump in her throat, unable to meet Pavane's pitying gaze.

'No cause is lost until it's been fought!' Rico intervened roughly. 'So just relax and enjoy your surroundings and let me work out the strategy!'

'Rico's right.' Pavane reached across the table to touch Merle's hand where it lay clenched on the table. 'Ever since he told me about you, I've been so looking forward to meeting you.

'While he's fighting it out with the lawyers you and I can go sightseeing and shopping, so at least whatever happens you won't return to England with totally unhappy memories, and this coming Sunday Armando will be back and my other brother-in-law Ramón and his family are visiting us from the Argentine, so we're throwing a big reunion party. You simply must be here for that!'

'Oh, but I don't think...' Unwilling to offend the other girl, whose genuine enthusiasm warmed her spirit, Merle hesitated, torn between her desire to fight for Paraiso to the bitter end and her longing to hold Laurie in her arms again. Besides, with the harsh feelings between herself and Rico so lightly veiled, to meet the rest of his family would be an impossible ordeal.

'Of course she'll stay.' Rico rose smoothly from the table, pushing back his chair, to come and stand behind her, resting his hands on her shoulders, automatically conjuring her troubled gaze to meet his own. 'Nothing could please me better than to introduce her to Armando. My brother has always been a superb judge of character and I'm sure he'll be enchanted with her.'

To Merle's shocked surprise his fingers lifted the heavy fall of bronze-black hair that splayed on her shoulders and came to rest on the nape of her neck, moving sinuously to caress the soft line of her throat. 'So let's say that's a definite appointment, eh, *querida mia*?'

It was a decision, although it had been voiced as a question, but as Merle's body tightened in defiance of his tyranny as much as against the liberties of his fingers, all thought of protest was banished from her mind as he dipped his sable head with elegant slowness to bestow a light kiss on her surprised mouth.

She sat speechless, embarrassed that he had touched her in front of his sister-in-law, giving such a wrong impression of the emotions that churned between them, yet unable to put the matter right. She knew only one thing: she was swimming well out of her depth in a pool the dangers and darknesses of which were well beyond her experience.

The shiver which traversed her spine had started on its unwelcome journey seconds before she heard Rico's voice, oozing with self-satisfaction, announcing smugly, 'Well, that's settled, then.'

It was with trepidation that Merle shook hands with Fidelio Diaz the following morning, her natural anxiety surfacing after a surprisingly restful sleep. She had been made so welcome at the *cortijo* the previous day, by the time night fell she had felt as if she had known and liked Pavane all her life! The presence of Elena and Nacio during the afternoon had probably accounted for Rico's relaxed attitude, she decided. He had been marvellous with them, demonstrating a limitless patience as they had clambered over him and involved him in their games. As with most Spanish men his affection for children was openly displayed, as was his pride in the fact that they were his brother's offspring, and heirs to the Montilla name.

Watching his gentleness, the sweetness of his smile, the power allied to the delicacy of his adroit hands, Merle had felt her heart lurch with the heady yet alarming emotion which had first assailed her a year earlier.

Lying in bed later, watching the pattern of moon-beams on the walls, she had realised with a shock that she had just spent one of the happiest days of her life since Rosemary's tragic and sudden death.

Rico's affability had still been in evidence at breakfast as he courteously enquired about her night's rest as if he really cared whether she had lain awake all night or found some respite in slumber.

Now, as the lawyer seated himself, Rico drew her down beside himself on the couch, taking the correspondence she had fortunately brought with her to Spain and passing it over to the older man.

'Is there anything you can do?' Her anxiety brought a tremor to her voice.

'It's a difficult situation, *señora—muy difícil...*' His face was stern, promising her no easy solution. No solution at all really, Merle recognised with painful perspicacity, as Rico's arm tightened supportively round her shoulders, before he addressed the other man in clipped Spanish.

There was no way Merle could understand the following exchange, neither did either man's businesslike tones convey anything to her. For all the use she was she might just as well have stayed in her room, she thought wearily.

At last it was over, Fidelio Diaz rising to shake her hand with studied courtesy, addressing her in her own language.

'I can promise you nothing, *señora*, apart from the fact that I will do my utmost on your behalf.'

She was grateful, of course, but it wasn't much to hold on to. Why on earth had she allowed herself to be talked into this diversion, she wondered miserably, when she could have been home with Laurie? Although she didn't question her decision to leave the little girl, especially in the present circumstances, it was the first time she had been parted from David's daughter since Rosemary had triumphantly brought her home from the maternity hospital. A wave of loneliness swamped her, destroying her composure, as she closed her eyes in an unsuccessful attempt to prevent her tears from spilling.

'*Fortaleza, mi amor*...our lawyer friend is too professionally reserved to raise your hopes, but I can assure you his best is very good indeed, and remember, the war isn't over until the last battle has been fought and won!'

Merle hadn't heard Rico re-enter the room after escorting their visitor to the front door, and she gave a little start of shock as his hand fell lightly on her shoulder as an accompaniment to his sympathetic words. It seemed he was exhorting her to show fortitude, although she was surprised he should address her as 'my love' in tones which showed compassion rather than the sarcasm to which she had grown accustomed.

Hastily she brushed the moisture from her cheeks, deciding there was little point in confessing that her tears had been because she missed Laurie rather than for the potential loss of Paraiso.

'In the meantime,' he was continuing briskly, 'the best thing you can do is to stop dwelling on your problems and try to enjoy yourself instead.' His gaze lingered speculatively on the plain pink cotton button-through dress she had chosen to wear for the morning's confrontation. 'So why don't you go and change into trousers and trainers and I'll take you for a ride through the estate?'

'You're very kind, but you don't have to entertain me.' Stiffly Merle refused his offer, not at all sure that being in his contentious presence would amount to much enjoyment! 'I want to phone my sister this morning, and afterwards I thought I'd help Pavane.'

'Phone by all means,' a dark brow rose in what she thought was faint amusement, 'since the advent of international subscriber dialling that will hardly take up much of your time, but as for helping Pavane, I can assure you my brother keeps an adequate staff for that purpose.'

'I thought you said she'd appreciate my company,' Merle challenged coolly.

'I don't deny it, but not this morning. Wednesdays are when she gives piano lessons to some of the children from the nearby village.'

'She's a music teacher!' It was impossible to hide her surprise. Somehow she hadn't expected Armando's wife to have a job.

Rico nodded. 'It was to be her career before she met and married Armando. Now it's her hobby, a way of passing on her talents to those less fortunate than herself. Rather than let her cancel her arrangements and disappoint the children, I've assured her that you and I will find plenty with which to amuse ourselves.'

'But what about Nacio and Elena...?' Some inner turmoil insisted she continued to oppose his suggestion, although reason prompted her that a tour of the estate in one of the *cortijo's* Jeeps would be instructive as well as enjoyable and she was being churlish to contend the suggestion.

Rico sighed impatiently. 'They have a perfectly good nurserymaid in Conchita. Today is one of the days she takes them to the village play-school. Now, are there any more obstacles you wish to erect? You want to write a letter, read a book, perhaps?'

His unqualified sarcasm brought the colour to her cheeks, aware as she was of her own ungraciousness. For a split second she even considered taking him up on one of his alternatives, but how could she concentrate on reading while the future of her investment lay in the balance? Besides, a breath of fresh air would do her a power of good.

'I wouldn't want to interfere with any plans you'd already made for yourself,' she returned stiffly.

'Good, that's settled it, then,' triumphantly Rico answered her querulous regard with a brilliant smile which lacked nothing but humour, 'since the only plan I had in mind for this morning was to pay a visit to an old friend of mine who's just got married, and has brought his wife here to introduce her to his family. As Esteban is staying with his father, who is Armando's farm manager and who has property on the estate, there's no problem.'

It was only because he disliked being thwarted rather than because her company was of paramount importance to him that Rico had been so adamant, Merle decided as a few minutes later she dragged on a pair of old blue denims, and topped them with a crisp shirt of blue checked cotton. Briskly she rolled the sleeves up above her elbows before brushing her thick hair and gathering it into a workmanlike ponytail. She didn't possess trainers, but she supposed an old pair of tennis shoes which were blissfully comfortable would suffice, although what had been wrong with her previous mode of dress she couldn't guess.

Rico was waiting for her in the hall as she moved lithely down the stairs, and she noted with some surprise that he, too, had changed, the light cotton trousers he had worn previously exchanged for black denims which highlighted the powerful musculature of his long legs. His broad shoulders now stretched the black cotton of a T-shirt, the rib of its short sleeves tightly encompassing the smooth bulge of his upper arms.

Her quickening pulse made her grab for the handrail as he stood, hands in his pockets, watching her descent.

Like an echo from the past a throbbing excitement held
her in its thrall, as she experienced for a fleeting second
the type of response she had once felt in his presence.
How stupid and untutored she'd been not to realise that
she had already been caught in a mire of dangerous
emotions, and flee from them before Rico had gone in
search of her that morning a year ago...

Meeting him again, she knew with a quiet desperation
that she had left it too late to raise defences against him.
She could only escape now when he chose to release her,
but he was proud and unforgiving, and unintentionally
she had aroused his antipathy. Too sensitive not to
discern that under the guise of helping her Rico's motives
were mixed, she knew that until that time came she would
have to pay the price of her foolishness in whatever coin
he demanded.

Almost unbearably conscious of the way Rico's dark
eyes glittered, sensually alive as they surveyed her chosen
outfit, Merle was determined he wouldn't guess the effect
he had on her. To offset the sudden weakness in her legs
and the unwelcome constriction in her throat she held
her head proudly high, refusing to enquire whether she
met with his approval as she reached ground level.

'That's much better!' He gave it to her anyway as if
it was of primary importance to her, continuing
smoothly, 'I've written out the international dialling code
for you on the phone pad. All you have to do is add
your sister's number.' He indicated the telephone en-
sconced on its own unit at one side of the expansive entrance hall. 'Take your time. I'll be waiting for you in
the *sala* when you've finished.'

Without waiting for her answer he turned on his heel
and strolled away. For a moment Merle paused, watching
his retreat, fighting down unbidden speculations: was
his body as marvellously tanned as it had been last year?

Was the smooth flesh of his back still seared with the brand of war? Was it just the awareness of his contempt that made his physical presence so actively disturbing to her?

From upstairs came the sound of children's laughter interspersed with Pavane's light tones—a sound that tugged at her heartstrings. What would Laurie be doing now? she wondered. She hoped she was not missing her as much as she missed her little stepdaughter. Resolutely she made her way to the phone and dialled Barbie's number.

Twenty minutes later she replaced the receiver, making a mental note to check how much she owed Pavane for the call. Barbara had been horrified at her news and intrigued by Rico's intervention. Not surprising, since she had told her sister very little about her previous encounter with the imperious Andalusian. Abruptly she had put an end to Barbie's speculations of romance, advising her sister that Rico was only acting out of a natural sense of justice and a wish that foreigners should see his country in a good light.

She smiled wryly to herself, imagining Barbie's reaction if she had told her Rico regarded her as a woman on the make—avaricious, disloyal and promiscuous! The only good news was that Laurie was well and happy. It had been wonderful to listen to the four-year-old bubbling on about the lovely time she was having with Natalie and how they'd been to a theme park and were looking forward to visiting a local zoo.

Rico was gazing out of the large windows at a terrace aglow with the colour of potted plants when Merle entered the *sala*. A slight lift of his dark brows demanded to know if her domestic affairs were in order and full explanations given and accepted. On her confirmation that everything was as settled as could be expected, he gave a satisfied nod and led her briskly outside.

Matching his stride, Merle followed in silence, too intent on enjoying the warmth of the sun on her bare arms and the spicy sweet scent of the atmosphere to pay much attention to their destination. It was with something of a shock that she came to a halt as Rico announced their arrival at the stables.

Stables! She had assumed they'd been walking towards a garage! Any hope that motorised transport awaited them was immediately dispelled as Rico continued forward across the cobbled yard, greeting the stablehand who hurried towards them.

'I'll take Zarina and Relámpago for a bit of exercise if they're fit.'

'*Por cierto*, Don Rico!'

Merle watched aghast as the lad moved towards some open stalls to return leading a horse by the bridle in each hand, a flush of mortification burning in her cheeks, more because of her misinterpretation of the word 'ride' than her lack of equestrian skills. How stupid she'd been not to put two and two together and realise the reason Rico had insisted she changed her dress!

'Rico...' she began.

'Mmm?' He had already thrown a blanket across the chestnut's back and stopped in the process of settling the saddle, to pay attention to her, his eyes narrowed against the glare of the sun. 'You've no objection to my choosing your mount, have you?'

'No...yes...' His impatient frown told her to be brief and specific. 'The thing is—I misunderstood you. I thought we were going by Jeep.' She took a deep breath. 'You see—I don't ride horseback!'

CHAPTER SEVEN

MERLE wasn't sure what reaction she had expected—irritation, disbelief, even annoyance that she'd spiked Rico's plans. What she hadn't anticipated was the careless shrug with which her statement was received as Rico returned to the task of tightening the girths.

'Then this is a marvellous opportunity for you to learn,' she was told calmly. 'Zarina is the most sweet-tempered mare that ever lived. She's sixteen years old and wise as befits her age. Believe me, she'll look after you with as much devotion as if you were her own foal!'

Merle swallowed unhappily. Sweet-tempered Zarina might be, but she was also large.

'Here...' Rico held out an imperious hand as, finishing his task, he rose to his full height and stroked the chestnut's copper nose. 'Come and make friends with her.' He paused as Merle hesitated. 'You're not afraid of horses, are you?'

'No, of course not!' Only of being astride their backs and out of contact with the ground, she might have added, but refrained from doing so. She moved forward boldly, allowing the mare to blow softly into her hand as she enquired doubtfully, 'But doesn't it take a long time to learn to ride?'

'If you wish to compete in the Olympics, undoubtedly. If you merely wish to ride around the *cortijo*, no time at all. The rules are simple. Here, let me help you mount and you'll see.'

She could refuse and risk his lifting her bodily into the saddle, or she could comply with good grace and hope for the best. The determination on his prepossessing face informed her that they were the only options open to her.

With as much dignity as she could muster Merle walked to Zarina's side and under Rico's instruction put her left foot in the stirrup.

'Fine,' he encouraged. 'Now grab the pommel on the saddle and swing your right leg up and over!'

It sounded easy, but Merle found herself lacking the confidence to put her full weight on the stirrup. Suppose Zarina moved? It was on her third attempt that Rico assisted her, placing his hands each side of her hips and thrusting her upwards so that she arrived on the saddle with a little gasp of surprise, as much at the feel of his firm hands placed so intimately on her body as from her sudden successful elevation. Comforted that beneath her Zarina remained as solid and stationary as a rock, she felt for the other stirrup, sighing with relief as her foot entered it effortlessly.

Beside her Rico mounted the large bay Relámpago with effortless athletic grace, reaching across to take Merle's reins, twist them into a circle and hand them back to her.

'A touch on the left rein and she'll go left, a touch on the right, right. Both together gently and she'll stop. To make her start press your heels in. The harder and more frequently you press the faster she'll go.'

'And that's all?' Merle asked faintly.

'For the moment.' Rico's beautiful mouth parted in a genuine smile as his eyes took in her rigid posture. 'The rest is common sense. You and the horse are a partnership and have to aid each other. When you go uphill lean your weight forward to distribute it. When you go downhill, lean backwards to balance the strain—

and, above all, relax. You're meant to be enjoying yourself!'

Fifteen minutes later Merle admitted she was. With Rico riding at her side and Zarina's sure-footed walk beneath her she had gradually gained confidence, her tight grip on the reins had loosened, her leg muscles had lost their tenseness and she was finding the leisurely transport through the leafy woods at the *cortijo*'s perimeter a stimulating experience.

'Am I going too slowly for you?' She turned concerned eyes to her companion, who was moving at the same pace, holding the reins loosely against Relámpago's back with one hand while the other rested lazily on one firmly muscled black-denim-covered thigh.

Rico's shapely mouth slanted her a mischievous grin for her solicitude.

'Do I take that enquiry to mean that you understand the translation of Relámpago's name?'

'No?' Merle raised enquiring brows.

Rico laughed, a natural expression of easy amusement that lightened her heart. 'He's called "Lightning", but that's because he was born in a thunderstorm rather than a reflection of the speed he can travel. But I'm quite content with our present pace. I can assure you I'm long past the wild days of my youth when I believed the only way to ride a horse or drive a car was at breakneck speed!'

The note of self-deprecation brought Merle's eyes back to his face, where she surprised a grimness of expression that made her heart beat a little faster. She knew so little about his early life, just the scant facts he had told her at their first meetings. A sudden need to gain his confidence prompted her to follow up his lead.

'You mean when you were still in the Argentine?'

'And afterwards.' Rico gave a short humourless laugh. 'I'm afraid I caused a certain amount of havoc when I arrived at the *cortijo*. In retrospect I'm amazed that Armando was as tolerant of my behaviour as he was!'

'It must have been a traumatic experience for you,' Merle pondered aloud. 'How old did you say you were—seventeen? Wouldn't it have been possible for you to study medicine in Argentina?'

'Theoretically, yes, of course.' He shrugged his shoulders, drawing her attention to the movement of their broad expanse beneath the dark shirt. 'In practice the truth was that my mother had just announced her plans to remarry and I didn't see eye to eye with her second husband-to-be. I was jealous that Mama had taken her attention from me to bestow on him and I resented his trying to take my father's place. As far as he was concerned, I was a thankless, selfish tearaway who had been thoroughly spoiled by a widow whose two eldest sons had returned to Spain, one to reclaim the heritage his father had neglected and the other to seek his fortune in Europe.'

'And were you?' Merle dared to ask, casting a sidelong glance at the stern profile beside her.

'Oh, yes indeed. The criticism was well merited, although naturally I didn't appreciate it at the time!' Dark eyes glowed with mocking self-knowledge and a hint of amusement, perhaps even pride, as Rico recalled his youthful exploits. 'Armando had always been very close to my father. I think Papa always regretted having neglected his Spanish property, but Mama would never dream of leaving South America, so Papa instilled in Armando the necessity of his reclaiming his inheritance one day and restoring it to its former glory. When Papa died, Armando would have stayed to look after Mama, but when she made it quite clear she preferred to return to her own family he felt free to leave her. My second brother, Ramón, decided to go with him. At the time Armando was just twenty and Ramón a year younger.'

'So you stayed with your mother?'

'Uh-huh. I was twelve, and for the next five years every whim I had was indulged. In Mama's eyes I could do no wrong, and I'm afraid I took every advantage of her complaisance! By the time I was seventeen and Mama broke the news to me that she was about to remarry, I'd become the leader of a small gang of youths whose sole aim in life was to live daringly. We rode too fast and drove too fast and boasted among ourselves of the conquests we'd made amongst feminine hearts!'

'I can imagine!' Merle interposed drily, finding no difficulty in envisaging a teenage Rico, blessed with fortune and good looks, idolised by his remaining parent and with no male control to guide his youthful exuberance. In all probability it wasn't only the female hearts he had captured but their bodies too, and it was only out of a courteous deference to herself that he had avoided making the point!

'In that case you can imagine too that I wasn't going to give up my lifestyle without a fight!'

'So what did you do? Challenge your prospective stepfather to a duel?' Merle wouldn't have put it past him. Rico aroused, she assessed, would stop at nothing to get what he wanted.

'No.' He offered her a contrite smile. 'I would feel prouder of my youthful self if I had. That, at least, would have been an honest action. Instead I was vain enough and stupid enough to try and force Mama to choose between the two of us. For some time, before I turned into a young savage, I'd been drawn to medicine as a profession and fortunately I'd done well enough in the sciences at school to make the possibility of medical school realistic. I told her that unless she gave up this idea of replacing Papa in her life I would follow Armando back to Spain and qualify there.' He gave a nonchalant shrug of his shoulders. 'You have a saying in English, I believe, about being hoist with one's own petard?' He invited her amusement with a lift of his dark brows.

Strangely Merle felt no delight at his humiliation. It was too easy to visualise Rico at seventeen, very proud and terribly vulnerable. His bluff called, he would have no recourse but to carry out his threat: leave his home and his doting mother to travel from one continent to another and place his future in the care of an older brother he hadn't seen for five years. The shock of his mother's decision must have hit him hard. How else could he have seen it but total rejection?

'It must have been a difficult time for you.' Merle's blue eyes darkened with sympathy as they dwelled on the lean face of the man riding beside her.

'Nothing more than I deserved.' He brushed aside her pity. 'My dislike of my stepfather was based on pure selfishness and an infantile possessiveness I felt towards Mama. There was no way we could have co-existed in the same house and he knew it. The truth is, he's a great guy, *muy hombre*, we would say, and he's made my mother very happy. After I'd qualified I went back to Argentina and made my peace with them—both of them.'

'I'm glad!' Merle spoke from her heart. What wouldn't she have given to be able to let bygones be bygones, but she hadn't needed her mother's warnings not to attempt a reconciliation. Her own intuition told her that neither she nor Barbie would ever be welcomed across the threshold of their own home while her stepfather still ruled it.

How hard it must have been for Rico to apologise for his youthful rashness, and how much she admired him for his action, guessing it couldn't have been without personal cost to his pride.

'Not as much as you undoubtedly will be to learn that we've arrived at our destination and you can dismount!' Rico cast her an amused look.

'Oh!' Merle had been so intent on her own thoughts, she hadn't realised that they had left the bridle path and were approaching an attractive white-painted hacienda, set in a fenced-off garden. 'As a matter of fact, I've enjoyed every moment of it!'

'Then it's my turn to say "I'm glad",' Rico nodded approvingly. 'You have a natural grace and carriage on horseback, a symbiosis with the animal which is very gratifying to watch. Within a few weeks you will be riding as well as I.'

'Except that I probably won't be here in a few weeks,' Merle returned sadly. 'In any case, even if miracles do happen I certainly won't be at the *cortijo*.'

'Oh, I don't know,' he contradicted her coolly. 'I'm sure my family would be only too delighted to meet yours. It occurs to me that your daughter must be about Nacio's age.'

'Laurie's four.' Even to her own ears Merle's voice sounded breathless, as her heart beat rhythmically faster. It had to be because of the graceful compliment he had paid her and the challenge of guiding Zarina towards the hitching post Rico was indicating to her. It couldn't be because of the way he'd looked at her just now, could it? She must have imagined the sudden unsullied glow of pure male appreciation in the slumbrous glance he'd levied at her.

Yet watching his casual dismount she felt every nerve in her body tingle with inexplicable anticipation. He made it look so easy, one hand steadying himself on the pommel as he swung the other high and wide across Relámpago's broad back.

For a split second it seemed that every muscle in the taut line of shoulder, buttock, thigh and calf was outlined beneath his clothes in splendid definition. Merle caught her breath in sheer admiration at the pure line of masculine beauty before her, the strength and resilience of God's ultimate creation casually displayed to heart-stopping effect. Dear heavens! What was happening to her? Her mouth dry, the perspiration breaking out on her forehead, she tried to forestall the sudden warm rise of blood to her face.

'It's not so difficult!' Rico had tied Relámpago to the post before coming to stand at her side, laughing up at her, his teeth a flash of white against the tanned darkness of his skin. 'Come, have confidence. You watched the way I did it, and I'll be here to catch you!'

Merle swallowed resolutely. Yes, she had watched him, but she had been thinking of other things than his technique. Gratefully she realised he had no idea her discomfort could be caused by anything other than her fear of leaving Zarina's back successfully.

Carefully she transferred her weight to the left stirrup, freeing her other leg. Gaining confidence as the mare stayed quietly in place, she swung her right leg up, but either she had misjudged the distance, or lacked Rico's athletic swing, because her heel dragged across the mare's back and, when she managed to get it clear, the ground seemed to be much further away than she'd judged. Her right leg buckled as it reached the ground and her hands fell from the pommel, leaving her left foot still in its stirrup.

'Careful!' She would have fallen if Rico hadn't held her firmly, his hands steadying her hips so she could disengage her foot.

'Well, I managed—after a way!' Triumphantly she turned in his arms to smile widely up into his dark eyes, the humour leaving her face as she read his purpose.

'Merle...' As his hands skimmed up her body to fasten around her shoulders, his words were little more than a sigh. 'Oh, Merle, how can I resist you?'

He didn't give her an opportunity of replying, as his arms tightened round her, pulling her hard against him, drawing her into his muscled frame. They were locked into a contact so intimate that their body heat mingled, and he bent his head to part the softness of her surprised mouth with his firm lips in a deep, searchingly ardent act of possession.

In his embrace Merle forgot everything—pride, self-respect, her resolution to keep their contact businesslike. Suddenly, with Rico's intimate caress on her lips, the passage of his hands branding her body even through the crisp cotton of her blouse, it was as if she had been transfixed by a magic spell, unable to do anything but respond to the invasion of her privacy with a delight that shocked her as much as it thrilled.

Even while her mind fought what was happening to her, her body was unashamedly glorying in the feel of Rico's powerful bones against her own, the sweet taste of his kiss, the highly erotic smell of clean sweat mingled with the lighter, tangier scent of some cologne and the aura of parched earth and grass beneath their feet.

She had never lain in a man's arms, or satisfied a man's lust. She had never been aroused by a man's touch or ached for fulfilment. For the first time in her life Merle was aware of her body's awakening; the stirring of desire; a muted hunger the pangs of which were painfully increasing; an unsuspected appetite that longed to feed from the grace and style of the clever, sensitive man who held her captive.

It was impossible! To give herself in a casual affair was utterly beyond everything she believed in, even if Rico had cared for her as a person. One day she might meet a man prepared to accept Laurie as his own child, a man she could respect as well as care for, a man who would like her as much as he desired her. In fact she hoped very much that she would. Ideally a child should have two parents, and Laurie had been most cruelly deprived. She owed this shadowy figure of her imagination her loyalty and her chastity. To indulge her own frailty with a man who saw her simply as a summer's pastime was unthinkable!

She opened her mouth in an attempt to put her thoughts into words when she saw Rico's glance flick behind her and felt his shoulders stiffen slightly.

The next moment he had taken her unresisting hands in his own and turned her so that she stood in front of him facing in the same direction. Instantly she realised why he had been distracted. Walking swiftly towards them was a man, probably a year or so younger than Rico himself, his face showing every sign of pleasure as he approached.

'Rico!' His hand went out in greeting. *'Estoy muy contento de verle!'*

'Esteban!' If there was a slight tinge of disappointment in Rico's voice Merle was the only one who heard it. *'Mi amigo!'*

The two men exchanged an arm clasp as Rico added in English, 'I'd like you to meet Merle, who is doing me the honour of staying with me at the *cortijo* for a few days.'

'I am delighted, *señorita*.' Esteban moved smoothly into barely accented English.

'Actually it's *"señora"*,' Merle corrected him awkwardly. 'My husband—that is...I'm a widow. But I'd really prefer you to call me Merle.'

'Con su permiso?' Dark eyebrows rose enquiringly as Esteban addressed Rico, a mocking smile on his lips.

The latter's mouth twisted in a wry grin. 'Certainly you have my permission, my friend, provided I am allowed to address your wife by her Christian name.'

'Ah, Isadora——' A shadow passed over Esteban's pleasant face. 'As a matter of fact I'm afraid she's not with me at the moment.'

'No?' Rico looked troubled. 'She's not unwell, I trust? I understood your purpose in coming here was to introduce her to your family.'

'Indeed it was, but things haven't worked out that way.' Esteban shrugged his shoulders. 'But allow me to explain over some refreshment in the house. My mother's very lonely now since the recent death of my grandmother, and with my father spending so many hours at the *cortijo*, she'll be delighted to see you—although,' he added with an apologetic glance at Merle, 'she has very little English.'

'Oh, please don't exclude her from the conversation on my behalf!' Merle interposed quickly. 'I shall be very happy listening to the three of you speaking in Spanish. It's a beautiful language and I have every intention of learning it when I—that is, if I ever come back here again.'

She was rewarded by a swift smile of thanks. 'You are *muy simpática*, Merle. My friend is a lucky man to have your companionship.'

'Indeed, yes,' Rico agreed suavely. 'Merle has been a constant delight to me since our first meeting a year ago.'

He placed a proprietorial arm around her waist as Esteban led the way to the hacienda, tightening his hold slightly as he felt her flinch involuntarily. Uneasily Merle glanced up at his strong profile, silently cursing her previous inability to repulse to him. It was clear from his whole bearing that he assumed she had welcomed his surrender to his baser nature. Well, she'd no one to blame but herself.

She could hardly envisage herself slapping his handsome face—the gesture would have been far too histrionic for her normally peaceable nature—but if she'd been able to gather her wits in time she could have told him in no uncertain terms that he would have to learn to resist her since she was definitely not available! It was an omission she would have to repair as soon as possible, she determined. In the meantime she must behave as distantly as she could without appearing too churlish.

In the event, it wasn't too difficult, as Esteban's mother Mariana made them welcome with a jug of *sangría* and a plateful of delicious *tapas*. Since the conversation was mostly in Spanish she accepted the fact of Rico's sitting beside her and holding her free hand, or occasionally putting his arm round her shoulders, with a good grace. Obviously he was ensuring that their hostess did not feel embarrassed by one of her guests being excluded.

In fact Merle found she was enjoying herself. The assortment of snacks was delicious and the wine cup cold and marvellously refreshing, so that she was surprised how quickly the time passed.

It was two hours later when Mariana excused herself to see to some household duties, and Esteban raised once more the question of his wife.

'We were all set to come here when Isadora heard from a friend of hers in Granada that she'd just given birth to her first child. As we were in this part of Spain she took the opportunity of visiting her and seeing the baby for herself.'

He didn't look too happy about the decision, Merle saw, and she could hardly blame him. Surely meeting one's in-laws was a greater priority than visiting a friend?

'Doubtless she'll be joining you soon?' asked Rico, sparing his friend a quizzical look.

'Certainly!' Esteban's reply was just a little too quick and to Merle's sensitive ear held an unnatural light-heartedness. 'I'm expecting her any day, and of course she'll be here in time for the party Pavane and Armando are throwing for Ramón's return!'

'Then I shall have to hold my curiosity in rein until then,' Rico said lightly. 'I must admit I'm intrigued to meet the woman who persuaded my old friend to give up his bachelorhood. I'd begun to believe you were finding the single life too full of opportunities to tie yourself to one woman.'

'We're not all as self-sufficient as you, my friend,' the younger man pointed out with a slight smile. 'And, while you no doubt spend many of your evenings reading learned medical journals, when I leave my office I leave my business worries in it.'

'Esteban runs a very successful company based in Barcelona designing and marketing ceramic tiles,' Rico advised Merle, before addressing the other man. 'Pavane mentioned something about your meeting Isadora through business, I believe?'

'She's a freelance interior-decorating consultant,' Esteban nodded, the pride in his wife's achievements clearly audible in his voice. 'We had to fit our wedding in between her commitments, which is why we didn't make a big fuss about it.' His pleasant face darkened as he rose to his feet and moved towards the window. 'I'm afraid that's something my parents find very hard to forgive, but, apart from having so little time to spare, Isadora hasn't any close family and she saw no reason to have anything other than a quiet ceremony.'

'I'm sure they'll forgive you both when they meet your wife,' Merle interposed sympathetically, addressing the young man's back. 'After all, it's the bride's prerogative to choose the kind of ceremony she wants on the day, isn't it?'

'Not if it takes place in Spain and excludes her husband-to-be's parents,' Rico commented drily. 'But Merle is right. I'm sure your wife is as charming and intelligent as she is undoubtedly beautiful. One look at her and she'll have Mariana and Enrico eating out of her talented hand!'

'I sincerely hope so!' There was heartfelt emphasis in Esteban's retort as he turned from the window. 'In fact, I'll drink to it! Pass the *sangría*, will you?'

It was just past midday when Merle remounted Zarina, delighted when she discovered she could do so without assistance, so much had her confidence increased.

'I thought we'd have a short ride through the fodder and grain fields before we turned for home,' Rico announced, having satisfied himself that she was securely and comfortably mounted. 'It's very pleasant up there and it'll give you some idea of the crops the farm produces. That is, unless you're stiffening up at all? I wouldn't want you to overtax yourself on your first ride.'

'No, I'm fine—honestly!' Merle turned eyes shining with happiness on him. She would never have believed the triumph she felt at accomplishing such a simple task as sitting on a horse while it ambled along beneath her. Of course, one couldn't call it riding as such, but it was a beginning. More to the point, she didn't feel at all stiff or tired. Probably because she had always been active her muscles were easily adaptable to new exercise.

The ride, as Rico had promised, was well worth taking, and she listened with interest as he explained that the farmland stretched over twelve thousand acres and was divided into different areas for different purposes, naming the various crops as they passed them.

It was about half an hour later that the cultivated parcels of land came to an end, to be replaced with open tree-dotted grassland.

'We can stop here and give our animals a breather,' Rico decided, narrowing his eyes to look at the broad clear expanse of azure sky over their heads. 'A little shade won't do us any harm either.'

He was right about that, Merle agreed silently, feeling the sun scorching her fair skin beneath the cotton of her blouse, and gratefully guiding Zarina in Relámpago's hoofmarks. She felt oddly lethargic—probably a combination of sunshine and *sangría* and the somnolent effect of her mount's gentle movement. Whatever the cause, when she tried to emulate Rico's clean dismount she found it impossible, hearing his soft laugh behind her as she struggled to clear Zarina's back with her plimsolled foot. A final effort had her making the same error she had made at the hacienda, stumbling back into Rico's arms.

For a few minutes she had forgotten the threat his presence posed her, the implications latent in that brief, interrupted embrace they had shared. Now they came sharply to the forefront of her mind, so that her whole body stiffened in his light hold.

CHAPTER EIGHT

'COME and sit down.' To Merle's relief Rico made no attempt to carry on where Esteban's appearance had interrupted them. Instead he led her towards the shade of a large tree, indicating where she should rest. 'Give me a few moments while I unsaddle the horses and lead them to some other shade, and I'll join you.'

Sprawling down on the surprisingly green turf, Merle watched Rico suit his actions to his words. There was a painful joy in watching the smooth muscular action of his body as he lifted the saddles off, placing them with the blankets in a neat pile beneath an adjacent tree.

Had she been a fool to allow him to bring her out here, so far away from the *cortijo*? Her mouth, dry already from the heat of the day and the mild alcohol of the *sangría*, became suddenly parched.

'What's the matter, Merle?' Every line of his intent face portrayed concern for her well-being as he approached her, a flask in his hand. 'Is the heat affecting you? *Dios*, I should have known better than to let you ride in the heat of the day without a hat!' He passed one hand through his own thick thatch of hair. 'I forget you're accustomed to colder climates. Here, have a drink from this. It's iced water Mariana gave me before we left.'

'Thank you.' Gratefully Merle accepted the flask, holding it to her lips and swallowing a couple of mouthfuls. 'I'm quite all right, really. Is it—is it safe to leave the horses like that without tying them up?' she pointed to where Zarina and Relámpago stood shoulder to shoulder, heads down nibbling at the grass, glad to have an opportunity to defer the reckoning of her unpredictable capitulation.

'Quite safe.' His tone teased her. 'You'll see I've pulled the reins down in front of them. They understand that means they are to stay where they are.'

'And they wouldn't dare to disobey you, I suppose?' An element of tartness had crept into her voice at his sublime faith in the creatures' behaviour.

'Not many people do,' Rico agreed easily. 'And they're both well trained and very contented where they are. Why should they wish to gallop away?'

'As long as you're happy...' Merle handed back the flask, watching as Rico lifted it to his own mouth, standing before her, head thrown back, the golden column of his throat strong and beautiful in the filtered sunlight.

'Oh, yes, I'm happy, Merle,' he answered her softly, dropping swiftly to her side to stretch out beside her in the welcome shade. 'Happier than I've been for a long while. Nearly as happy as I was last year before I found out that you didn't consider a husband an obstacle to enjoying yourself.'

'Oh!' For a moment she had forgotten the recrimination that lurked beneath the surface of his pleasantries.

'No, don't be upset, *mi amor*,' he instructed swiftly. 'Oh, I don't deny I was hurt and angry when I found out you were married. And when I saw your husband was so much older than you all I could think of was that you could only have married him because of the material things he could give you.' His mouth twisted in a wry smile that lacked humour. 'Not that I've anything against that in principle. All marriages are basically for selfish reasons, even if they're based on "the exchange of your true love for mine"!' He turned a thoughtful look on her distressed face. 'I just happen to believe that all contracts should be honoured, not just those concerning bricks and mortar.'

'I can't—I won't listen to this!' However much she might be in his debt, she wouldn't sit through these cruel aspersions against her character. 'There's no point in repeating what you thought——'

'Oh, but there is!' As she tried to rise Rico turned towards her, pinning her back on to the ground with swift motion. 'Because I think I understand now. It was security you were looking for. *Dios*, Merle! Ever since you told me about your childhood, the way that love was withheld from you, it's been becoming clearer and clearer in my mind. You weren't just looking for a rich husband, you were looking for a father figure to give you the love you were deprived of when you were young. But you'd never known what it was like to love and be loved. You didn't know what you would be missing, did you, *querida*?'

'You're wrong,' she interjected harshly, trying unsuccessfully to escape Rico's impassioned hold. How dared he try and evaluate her motives in an attempt to rationalise his own behaviour—whitewashing what he still despised to justify his own desire for the imperfect? Her voice shook. 'What gives you the right to try and analyse me? I thought you were a bone surgeon, not a psychiatrist!' Angrily Merle sprang to her own defence, pleased when she saw his jaw tighten at her indictment and knew her barb had met its mark.

'I'm the man who wants to become your *amante*— your lover: the man whose dreams you've haunted for the past year.' Rico drew in a harsh breath. 'Whatever happened in the past, you're free now: free to take and enjoy what you desire...'

'And you think that's you?' His face was so close to her she could see the texture of his skin and feel his breath on her cheek, perceive the tingling of her nerve-ends below the surface of her skin, as she recognised with an aching desperation that his audacity would have been more bearable if it had been less well founded!

'Isn't it?' he asked gently, dark eyes soft with beguilement as they surveyed her hostile face. 'When I hold you in my arms and taste your sweet kiss I believe it is.'

'Then you're fooling yourself!' Gathering her strength, Merle pushed herself up on her arms, relieved when Rico allowed her to rise to her feet. She brushed fragments of grass off her jeans, not prepared to meet his pensive gaze as she told him shakily, 'The fact is you've taken me by surprise once or twice and I've . . . I've responded automatically.'

'Oh, delicious automation!' Cynicism burned in the deep timbre of his quick retort. 'Oh, faithless Merle who will give her favours at any man's touch!'

'You're deliberately misinterpreting what I mean!' she flared back angrily. 'Ever since we met again you've been teasing me for your own pleasure . . .'

'You do me an injustice, *mi amor*. Although I find the prospect of doing so an entrancing one, I can assure you I haven't even started yet—and when I do you won't be in any doubt about it.' Rico rose easily to his feet.

'You speak as if I won't have any say in the matter.' Her blue gaze flicked contemptuously over his gracefully lounging figure, her voice low and well controlled despite the increased beat of her heart. 'Where I come from a man who forces his attentions on an unwilling woman is considered a criminal at the most, a lout at the least!'

Merle saw his expression harden and wondered if she'd gone too far, stepping back as he moved forward and caught her roughly by the arm.

'Here too, *querida*,' he clipped out softly but vehemently, 'we have a great respect for virtuous women, women who honour themselves and their men! But by the same token we are not always averse to indulging the passions of the flesh when they are freely offered outside the bounds of matrimony!'

'And when they're refused?' she challenged boldly, feeling her blood change to water as his fingers moved gently on her upper arm.

'Why do you deny the attraction between us, Merle?' Rico had chosen to ignore her question, asking his own instead. 'Last year you were ready to flirt with me, encourage me to believe you wanted me as badly as I wanted you. Now suddenly you're denying it with your lips, yet when I'm close to you I can feel you tremble. Am I to believe it's fear and not desire, hmm?' His other hand moved to trace a line down her cheek, while she stood mesmerised by his dark intensity. 'Ah, no. You know too well I'd never hurt you deliberately. Why go on punishing me, then? Is it because I left you so suddenly?'

Wordlessly Merle shook her head. More than anything else in the world at that moment she wanted to take him in her arms, cradle his head against her breast and feel his strong heart beating against her own. Still some remnants of self-respect held her back. In Rico's eyes she was 'easy' and available. To go to him on those terms would cheapen both of them, and she knew she must fight the growing temptation that was threatening her resolve.

She heard him sigh, felt its aftermath pass through his frame. 'Do you think it was easy for me to go like that? To pack my bags and disappear without seeing you once more, without feasting my eyes on your lustrous eyes and smoky hair, without hearing your soft voice and seeing your tremulous smile again. Do you Merle?'

The soft words flowed over her, caressing her with compliments, attacking her already weakening resolve. Somehow she had to find the strength to hold to her convictions, and the best way was in attack!

'Easy?' she echoed the word, lifting her delicate eyebrows and allowing the niggling pain caused by his disparagement to surface. 'Yes, since you ask, I would think you found it very easy. With such a well developed sense of morality I imagine you drove away on a cloud of virtue that cushioned you against any temporary disappointment.'

'Devastation,' he corrected softly. 'Devastation, not disappointment, and certainly not temporary. The discovery of your *desenfreno*——' He saw her frown of puzzlement at the Spanish word and sought for a translation with an impatient exhalation of breath. 'You would say "wildness—lack of restraint", I believe. The discovery of it has burned in my memory since I saw the evidence of it with my own eyes.' His voice deepened, developed a husky note. 'It wasn't the first time, you see. Once before I'd had the misfortune to imagine myself in love with a married woman, but on that occasion I'd known she had a husband before we became lovers...'

'Rico...' Shocked by the pain on his face, Merle made an involuntary movement towards him. 'You don't have to tell me...'

'I think I do.' He spoke with a quiet emphasis, brushing her protest away with a sharp movement of his hands. 'If only to stop you regarding me as some pious celibate who has never known the fires of the flesh!' He paused, swallowing before continuing matter-of-factly, 'It happened many years ago, shortly after I arrived in Spain. I could try to make excuses—tell you I was lonely and unhappy, that I was finding medical school hard work and it didn't help my confidence when the other students laughed at my South American accent.' He smiled deprecatingly, a soft turn of his lips that made Merle's heart seem to turn over. 'I could confess I missed my mother's adoration and the plaudits of my old friends. As I told you earlier, I was a typically spoiled young man feeling that the world owed me a living... None of which exonerates me for what I did. *She*...' he paused again as if collecting his thoughts, while Merle watched sadness shadow the clear sparkle of his eyes, '...she was going through a bad patch in her marriage. She needed help and understanding, and she came to me for them because she didn't want to talk to a priest, and as a trainee doctor I was the next best thing in her estimation.'

'And you took comfort from each other,' Merle said softly, compassion for his obvious distress lending her tone a husky depth.

'Yes.' His dark head dipped in acknowledgement. 'To my eternal shame, we did. I betrayed her confidences and her trust. Instead of being strong I acted like a weak simpleton...and then...her husband became suspicious...'

'Dear heaven!'

Merle didn't need the danger of that situation being spelled out to her, her fingers automatically curling into her palms in fearful expectation, as Rico continued roughly. 'If the true facts had been found out so many lives could have been ruined. Her husband's, hers, my family's...'

'And yours...'

'Mine, too.' He gave a poor imitation of a smile, the agony still sharp behind his eyes. 'In the event I paid a painful enough price for my indiscretion, but nothing more than I deserved—and of course I lost the girl... It was only thanks to some speedy action by Armando and Pavane that the true facts were never made public, and her husband was eventually persuaded to believe that my lover was another woman who couldn't be hurt by the scandal.'

'Her husband—he avenged himself on you before your brother intervened?' The reference to a painful price could surely only refer to physical retribution, and the thought made Merle shudder as she found herself unable to refrain from asking the question.

'Does the thought please or concern you, I wonder?' Rico cast her a speculative glance from sombre eyes. 'If the former then you can be assured he spared no effort in making his displeasure felt, and, since I had no heart to defend myself against his righteous wrath, I was lucky to escape with all my faculties intact.' He paused as if trying to read her expression, then went on equably, 'If the latter, then I can promise you I suffered no lasting physical harm.'

'Did you love her very much?' An unaccountable pang of jealousy lanced through Merle as painful as a rapier thrust.

'At the time I believed so.' Rico shrugged his shoulders. 'I was very young and very impressionable. You might say that the experience made me grow up overnight. Particularly when I saw my ex-lover's marriage begin to thrive again and realised I'd only been used as a substitute for the husband she had truly loved all along!'

'I'm sorry.' They were plain little words to explain how deeply she understood and sympathised with his suffering.

Again that barely perceptible movement of his broad shoulders. 'Perhaps you'll understand now why I reacted so strongly when I discovered that for the second time in my life I'd been travelling down a forbidden path, and this time, unknowingly! You set me up, Merlita, with your innocent eyes and breathy sighs, your smiling lips and gentle hands.' The dark gleam of his eyes was intense through the narrowed lids. 'I believed you were offering me the only pleasure in the world I craved——'

'No!' It was a cry of anguish wrung from her dry throat, as guilt tortured her. He would never believe she had been stupid rather than wanton! 'I wanted——'

'The best of both worlds—I know!' Rico reached for her, drawing her unresisting body against his own, staring down into her pale face. '*Santa madre de Dios*, and who am I to judge you? There is nothing, no one now to stand between you and your need for love.' He lowered his head, but she jerked her face away so that his seeking lips brushed against her cheek.

'You're not talking about love—what you mean is carnal appetite—animal desire...' she accused angrily.

'Do I?' There was a breath of laughter in his voice, a wicked promise in his expression that had her pulling away from him, only to find herself backed up against the wide trunk of the tree which had been her protector from the sun.

Immediately Rico's arms left her body to rest palm outward against the tree, effectively imprisoning her. With his body still in such close contact a wave of desire flooded through her system. Horrified at her own weakness, she recognised a desperate ache to pull him even closer, an impulsive urge to wind her fingers through the glossy hair on his formidable head, to seek and return his soft kisses with an ardour which should both shock and delight him, as his dark-pupilled eyes rested on her face, drowsy with supplication.

It wasn't fair. She was having to fight both of them. If only she was able to ignore the persistent murmur from her subconscious mind which was telling her over and over again that, although pity might be akin to love and her compassionate nature had responded to Rico's story of forbidden romance, it wasn't pity which held her enthralled in his company! It wasn't sympathy which had set her pulse into overdrive, sent the blood thrumming through her veins and weakened the muscles of her legs so greatly that it was all she could do not to throw herself against the strong body which prevented her escape and beg for support. She loved Rico de Montilla.

She had never gone through the throes of calf-love, never been infatuated by pop stars of TV actors. All her life until now her heart had been encased in ice where the opposite sex had been concerned. It had taken the heat of Andalusia and the stunning presence of the man in front of her to reach through that frigid barrier and begin to show her the depth of her own sensuality. Wearily she recognised that the process had started a year ago, only she had been too blinded by her immediate problems to acknowledge it.

Only her pride now stood between Rico and her unconditional surrender, and she would make every effort to preserve it.

As if guessing her inner turmoil, Rico slackened the rigid length of his restraining arms, allowing himself to seek her soft cheek with his questing lips. The sensation was devastating, generating a response she could barely understand and only control with enormous difficulty.

Inhaling sharply, Merle closed her eyes, making no attempt to repulse him. He was reading her as experienced and disillusioned, ripe for picking and enjoying, so that the physical pleasure of his touch was sullied, contaminated by his poor opinion of her.

'Merle, oh, Merle...' He had sought and found her trembling mouth, whispering her name against soft lips. 'It was Fate that brought us together again...'

It was then Merle knew what she must do. She must become the mercenary, heartless woman whose ethics he deplored while he still hungered for the relief and comfort of her body. Raising her hands to his face, she gently pushed him away, mutely praying for the confidence to carry her plan through.

'Tell me, Rico,' she asked softly, 'why did you bring me here? Do you really have any intention of getting Paraiso back for me, or did you intend all the time to seduce me?'

'I don't regard the two things as mutually exclusive.' Rico regarded her quizzically. 'I can assure you Fidelio Diaz will be working on the problem, if that's what's worrying you.'

'Mmm...' Merle raised her hands to his shoulders fending him off as he would have moved closer to her. 'I seem to remember you recently told me you found the grass on the other side trampled and unattractive?'

To her utter astonishment he actually had the grace to blush, a dull tide of colour climbing his jaw to confirm his embarrassment.

'A remark that was ungallant and uncalled-for...and untrue. Since then I've not only discovered that you are no longer married, but I can understand better your reasons for acting as you did. The truth is I——'

'The truth is your first estimation of my motives for marrying David was perfectly accurate.' Commanding every last gram of her courage, she met his regard without blinking, lying in the cause of self-preservation. 'He was a wealthy man and I was tired of being poor. You seem to think I'm the kind of woman who'll tumble into bed with anyone who asks her. Well, you're wrong! I don't deny you're attractive, but if I had an affair with every good-looking man who asked me then I would deserve your contempt!'

'Merle!'

The laughter had left Rico's face as she ignored his protest, continuing doggedly, 'I don't give anything away for nothing—I never have.' She paused, her breasts rising and falling rapidly in her agitation. 'I'm quite happy for us to become lovers...' she glimpsed and momentarily enjoyed the triumph that blazed across his face before adding '...the day you give me the key to Paraiso.'

'I see.' He smiled slowly, his gaze travelling over her in a way that sent the warm blood pouring into her face. 'No pleasure without business—that's the message, is it?

Merle nodded, not trusting herself to speak. The odds against Fidelio Diaz's accomplishing anything constructive had always been long. In a day or so when he reported back the failure of his undertaking she would be able to return to England, if not heart-whole at least without the agonising memory of the knowledge of Rico's magnificent body to torment her. And if Diaz succeeded? a tiny inner voice demanded. Why, then she would keep her word and Rico would never know she had given him her heart as well as her body. That way she could hold her head high when she left. They would have met and loved as equals, and he would never dream how absolutely he had conquered her.

'So...' He stepped away from her, his composure apparently undisturbed by her revelation of her supposedly mercenary heart—but then she'd only confirmed what he'd already suspected, hadn't she? 'You certainly put a high price on your favours, or can it be you doubt the success of my mission? I do hope it's not the latter, because I don't give up anything easily, *querida*, and I regard a bargain as a bargain.'

'Good.' Merle was proud of her bearing as she moved past him, her head high. 'Now we understand each other so well, perhaps we should be returning to the *cortijo*?'

'*Por cierto.*' He followed her lead, moving towards the blankets and saddles and beginning methodically to resaddle their mounts while she watched him, her heart heavy with despair. She allowed her eyes to linger on Rico's elegantly muscular body as he tightened the girths on Zarina with brisk efficiency. He might feel frustrated now, but he wouldn't be without female company for long, she was sure.

She sensed that she was the first person Rico had opened his heart to so fully, expunging the guilt and bitterness of the past. With luck it would leave him purged of remorse, enabling him to discover true love instead of mere sensual satisfaction. Doggedly she ignored the pang of grief which accompanied the belief.

'Shall we go?' His voice was as expressionless as his face as he offered her his help to remount.

'Thank you.' His hands had stayed in contact with her only as long as necessary to see her safely in the saddle.

At the very least she had earned herself a respite from his provocation, she consoled herself reading the coldness that hardened his profile as he turned away. It was a pity the realisation didn't fill her with the exultation she had expected.

After the silence of the ride back to the *cortijo* Merle was relieved when they reached the farm and she was able to relax temporarily in the sanctuary of her room.

Pavane had met them on their return to say that lunch would be ready as soon as they wished on the terrace surrounding the swimming-pool. A tepid bath would have been a pleasant way of indulging herself, but rather than keep her hostess waiting Merle settled for a shower before surveying her wardrobe. Something cool was called for, and a little sun on her pale skin wouldn't do much harm if she applied sun milk lavishly.

Quickly she decided on rose-pink cuffed shorts with a matching print vest top, grimacing slightly as she caught sight of her pale legs in the long mirror. At least they were long and shapely, which did something to offset their winter pallor, she supposed, smiling inwardly at her own vanity.

Sliding her bare feet into a pair of white wedge-heeled mules and with her hair cascading softly to her shoulders—a sure protection on the tender nape of her neck against the burning kiss of the early afternoon sun—she hurried down the superb staircase and out on to the patio.

Pavane and Rico were already seated at a long table beneath a flowered canopy when she arrived beside the pool, having made her way round the side of the *cortijo*. There were two pools, one kidney-shaped, the other a circular child's pool with a small fountain in the centre.

'Have I kept you waiting? I'm so sorry!' She hurried forward.

'Of course not.' Rico rose leisurely to his feet, the epitome of elegant courtesy. 'Our time's entirely our own and the meal's a cold one.' He pulled the remaining wrought-iron, sumptuously padded chair away from the table with the practised ease of a head waiter, as Merle murmured her thanks.

As he bent considerately over her, easing the chair back into place as she took her seat, Merle caught the citrus-fresh tang of his still-damp hair. He too had changed his clothes, she saw. Of course it had to be coincidence, but she could have sworn he was wearing the identical outfit he had had on when she had first set eyes on him.

Whether he had intended it or not, she felt an almost unbearable twinge of sweet remembrance at the sight of his unclad legs, muscularly golden beneath the short white shorts, and the expensively thin short-sleeved shirt worn casually open to display the firm unblemished skin of his chest and diaphragm. Finding herself wondering if the marks of war that laced his back had faded with the passing months, she made a conscious effort to drag her mind away from such disturbing contemplation, to concentrate on the present.

The table was laden with covered dishes which were opened to reveal an assortment of cold meats and exotic mixed salads. One wicker basket contained chunks of delicious French-style baguette while a large silver tureen encased in a bowl of ice cubes was filled with a luscious gazpacho.

Merle felt her appetite reviving just at the sight of the simple but beautifully prepared and served food, helping herself eagerly as invited and accepting a glass of ice-cool Spanish champagne from Rico.

'To us and the success of our endeavour!' He smiled across the table at her, lifting his champagne flute towards her so she had no option but to clink her glass against his, intensely aware that his bold dark eyes were toasting something quite different from the obvious.

'I'll drink to that!' Pavane touched her own glass against her brother-in-law's and her guest's before taking a deep sip and leaning earnestly across the table towards Merle. 'We've had a marvellous idea!' Her blue eyes sparkled with enthusiasm. 'After lunch you must phone your sister and invite her to bring your little girl and her own family over here for the holiday they've been looking forward to. They can stay in the Villa Jazmin for as long as they like as our guests!'

'Oh, but——' Sheer surprise struck Merle dumb.

'It's perfect, don't you see?' Pavane enthused happily. 'Everyone gains. You'll be reunited with Laurie—and I know how you must be feeling. Armando insisted I went into a maternity hospital for Elena's birth in case there were complications, and I couldn't wait to get back to Nacio. Your sister and her family won't be deprived of a holiday I'm sure they've been looking forward to, and you yourself will be able to stay here until we know something definite about Paraiso without eating your heart out for Laurie!'

'But what about Rico?' Too stunned to know exactly how she felt, Merle turned questioning eyes to the sombre face of the man opposite her. 'It's your summer retreat. I couldn't expect you to move out.'

'On the contrary, if you cast your mind back you'll remember that Jazmin belongs to the estate and is in my brother's gift.' There was no indication in Rico's bland expression as to how he had received Pavane's suggestion, but any doubt Merle might have harboured regarding his approval of the plan was immediately dispersed by his sister-in-law's interjection.

'Actually it was Rico's idea, though why I didn't think of it myself I'll never know. Oh, you must agree, Merle! There can't possibly be any reason for refusing, can there? It comes with an excellent maid service. The whole place can be restocked with food, cleaned and made ready in a matter of hours. Just think of it, this time the day after tomorrow you could all be on the beach together just as you'd originally planned. Even if, heaven forbid, Rico and Diaz can't do anything about Paraiso at least you'll all have had the holiday you planned.'

Playing for time, Merle drank a deep draught of champagne. How ironical that she should receive such an invitation when she'd just been considering escaping from the heady atmosphere of Rico's presence by returning home!

'How about Armando?' she asked, carefully replacing her glass on the table. 'Will he be prepared to let the villa out to strangers?'

'Rest assured, my brother's a total slave to his wife's desires, though neither would publicly admit the fact.' Rico exchanged a look of deep affection with his lovely sister-in-law as she contented herself with a soft smile and a tiny shake of her head. 'But I can assure you of two things, the first is that neither Pavane nor myself regard you as a stranger, the second is that Armando would never "let" Jazmin. It's there for the benefit of his friends and employees, and as far as he's concerned, my friends are his.'

'I don't know...' Merle began a little desperately. It would mean another two weeks of leaving herself open to the disquieting effect Rico had on her... On the other hand, would it? Perhaps with her family occupying Jazmin he would return to Cadiz. In any case, if he spent time at the *cortijo* he would be well away from the coast. He could hardly harass her from that distance, could he? And Barbie and Grant deserved a holiday. All her sister's sympathy had been for her, Merle, when she had broken the news to her, but she didn't need to be psychic to know how disappointed Barbie must have been on her own account. For weeks now she had been shopping around compiling what she called 'a hot-weather wardrobe'. How could she turn down such an opportunity to give Barbie the pleasure she'd promised?

CHAPTER NINE

'WHAT'S the problem, Merle?' Rico's soft question interrupted her deliberations. 'Is it that you find our hospitality lacking in some respect?'

'Of course not!' His carping words spurred her to speech. 'I can't begin to thank Pavane for allowing me to come here, and as for you...' She paused, drawing in her breath, trying to salvage something from the morass of emotions she was experiencing for the taunting Andalusian who continued to regard her with barely veiled irony.

'As for me...?' he prompted gently.

In front of Pavane Merle could hardly say anything uncomplimentary, and in truth she had to acknowledge a debt to Rico. Without his help she would already be back in England, sadder, wiser and poorer, without even the faintest glimmer of hope.

'As for you,' she continued smoothly, 'I hope I can find some way of recompensing you for all the trouble you've already taken on my behalf,' and dared him with sparkling eyes to say one word out of place.

'Your continued presence here is reward enough,' he told her gallantly, but the chivalry in his soft tone was belied by the sudden flash of naked warfare that dilated his pupils. 'Do you wish me to beg you to stay?'

'No, of course not.' The thought of Rico prostrate at her feet was more than she could bear, and she wouldn't put it past him to subject her to such an embarrassment. 'I'll phone Barbie after lunch.'

'Splendid!' Rico refilled her glass. 'Finish your salad and I'll go and tell Ana that we're ready for dessert and coffee.'

He pushed his chair away from the table, suiting his actions to his words, striding with lazy power towards the kitchen.

'I'm so glad you're staying.' Genuine warmth echoed in Pavane's soft tones. 'And I know Rico is delighted!'

It wasn't the word Merle would have chosen herself, but certainly Rico was at his most charming for the remainder of the meal, which consisted of crunchy meringue and cherries laced with kirsch with a dressing of whipped cream and aromatic coffee served in a *cafetière*. For those relaxing, blissful moments she could almost imagine he was once more the man she had met and been entranced by on a lonely beach on the Costa de la Luz so many months before.

An hour later, after an excited exchange of news with Laurie—who, fortunately, didn't appear to be missing her at all!—she was listening to Barbie's squeal of joy echoing over the phone wires. 'Merle darling! Oh, how marvellous! Of course we'd love to come. Grant's working until Saturday because we weren't sure what was happening, but if we can get a flight we could be with you this coming Sunday, would that be OK?'

'Sunday?' Merle repeated the word, turning raised eyebrows for approval towards Pavane, who was waiting beside her in the hallway.

'Lovely!' Armando's wife nodded. 'Ask her to let you know in advance which airport she'll be using and we'll arrange for her to be picked up and brought directly here. That way you can all meet Armando and be at Ramón's welcome home party, stay the night and we'll take you over to Jazmin the next day.'

'Oh, but surely...' Clapping her hand over the mouthpiece, Merle demurred. 'There'll be five of us altogether. You can't cope with all that extra work!'

'Merle, are you still there?' Barbie's voice sounded querulously in her ear.

'Here—let me.' Pavane held out a slim hand for the phone. With a despairing shrug of her shoulders Merle handed it over, standing by helplessly as arrangements were neatly taken out of her hands.

'That's settled,' Pavane said with satisfaction, replacing the receiver after a ten-minute conversation. 'Believe me, it's entirely in my own interests. If your sister arrives on Sunday and goes straight to Jazmin you'll go with her, and Rico will never forgive me for allowing you to go without meeting Armando first. They may have had their disagreements in the past, but these last few years they've grown a lot closer, finding a mutual respect for each other.'

Love for her husband endowed Pavane's face with an inner radiance, the source of which was unmistakable, causing Merle's breath to catch in her throat.

'Are they very much alike—Rico and your husband?' she asked with a sudden desperate need to know what it was Armando possessed to capture and hold a woman as lovely as the one who now turned eyes bright with emotion to survey her.

'Yes.' The reply was without prevarication. 'Both are proud and handsome, idealistic and charming, hard as steel when the mood takes them, yet soft as the hair on Elena's pretty head when the moment's right.' Pavane looked thoughtfully at her guest. 'Someone once said to me "never fall in love with an Andalusian! They're volatile, graceful, charming and ardent lovers—but they make deadly enemies and they can break a woman's heart

with impossible cruelty," all of which is true, but...'
her smile was secret, turned inwards towards her own
memories '...but that same quality which makes them
so rigid and unbending can also, when they fall in love,
turn them into devoted husbands whose generous and
passionate love can make every day into a celebration
of life! But there, I admit it. I'm prejudiced!'

Prejudiced she might be, but there was no doubt that
Pavane's marriage was idyllic. Lying on her soft bed,
the blinds half shuttered so that the slanting rays of the
sun fell in zebra-like stripes across her half-naked body,
Merle felt an aching envy for her hostess's glowing
happiness.

She had chosen to rest rather than join Rico in the
pool after lunch, making the excuse that her legs were
beginning to ache after the morning's exercise. The truth
was that the ambivalent feelings she was experiencing in
Rico's company were becoming difficult to bear with
equanimity. Distance, she had told herself firmly, would
lend enchantment to her present position. Today was
only Wednesday and it would be another four days before
she could escape the effects of the electrically charged
aura he seemed to generate around her.

Suppose she had been single when they had met? That
she had never known David or Laurie? Would the same
attraction have blazed between them? And if so, what
would have been the outcome? She stirred languidly as
the breeze through the shutters fanned her warm cheeks,
and her imagination wandered freely, still continuing to
function long after sleep had claimed her, weaving its
fantasies into her dreams.

A light tap on the door brought her back to wakefulness. Quickly holding the bedcover to her chest, she
bade the visitor enter.

'I thought you might be able to use a cup of tea.' It was Pavane who came in, putting a cup and saucer on the bedside table.

'Lovely!' Gratefully Merle took a sip, allowing the bedcover to drop into her lap. 'What time is it?'

'Six.' Pavane smiled at her guest's horrified face. 'You've had quite a long siesta.'

'Heavens!' She should have realised that sunshine and champagne mixed could have a super-tranquillising effect. 'You must think me awfully rude.'

'Of course not, you're entirely free to do as you wish.' Any embarrassment Merle felt was dispersed by the other woman's friendly denial. 'I just came to tell you that dinner will be at eight tonight. Rico's gone over to see Esteban and I've invited him to join us this evening. I imagine he's feeling a bit depressed with Isadora still away.' For a moment the smile died from her face, to be replaced with a thoughtful frown before she brightened again. 'Come down whenever you're ready, I'll be on the patio with the children. It's lovely out there now, not too hot, and we can have a chat over pre-dinner sherry.'

Left alone, Merle sipped the tea while bringing herself slowly back to a state of complete wakefulness. Taking her time in getting ready, she applied a light foundation to her creamy skin, touching it with a puff of powder sufficient to remove any shine, before turning her attention to her eyes. She used eyeshadow sparingly, applying neutral shades to highlight the lid and deepen the socket area. In the soft light of the bedroom her eyes seemed enormous, the lashes already dark, but discreetly thickened with mascara forming a silkily lush frame around them.

From somewhere outside on the patio came the sound of light classical music as Merle traced the perfect outline of her mouth with a soft pink lipstick, deciding at the last moment to seal it with a coat of gloss. What to wear? Thoughtfully she surveyed the choice available, eventually selecting a full-skirted dress of emerald silk, simply cut with a boat-shaped neckline and tiny cap sleeves which just covered her shoulder-bones. Lastly she slipped her feet into high-heeled black sandals, pausing to survey her reflection in the mirror on her way to the door. Yes, she decided critically, she looked as good as she could reasonably hope to, and the added sparkle in her eyes and lift to her walk was undoubtedly due to the expectation of her imminent reunion with Laurie...

'What a lovely dress!' Pavane cast admiring eyes over Merle as she joined mother and children. 'I remember I wore one just the same colour shortly after I married Armando.' The compliment was obviously genuine, the memory apparently reawakening some tender emotion from the past, if the other girl's reminiscent smile was anything to go by.

'Thank you.' Merle sank gracefully down on the swinging hammock, to be immediately approached by Elena demanding to sit on her lap. The time passed so quickly after that, what with amusing the children and exchanging news and views with Pavane, the arrival of Rico and Esteban took her by surprise.

Dinner was served in the *sala*—a pleasant meal accompanied by fine Spanish wines, which Merle partook of with caution, not wishing to fall asleep before the evening was over. Pavane proved a charming and accomplished hostess, the conversation flowing easily among the four of them, although to Merle's perceptive eye Esteban's gaiety seemed rather forced and his appreciation of the wine somewhat indiscreet.

Although Elena had gone to bed before the meal began, Nacio had been allowed to join the adults for the first hour, behaving himself with a maturity far beyond his years and winning Merle's unqualified admiration.

Relaxing afterwards on one of the luxurious leather couches, Merle, having turned down the offer of brandy or liqueur with her coffee, was only too pleased to indulge herself with one or two *petits fours*, as Pavane, in answer to Rico's request, seated herself at the grand piano at the far end of the room and played Beethoven's Pathétique Sonata. Beside her on the couch, Esteban stared down unblinkingly into the depths of his brandy glass as if it held the answer to some insurmountable problem, while Rico, sprawled in an easy chair with his eyes closed, absorbed the beauty and technique of his brother's wife's performance as the music sprang to life beneath her able fingers.

'I'm sorry to interrupt, Doña Pavane, but the baby is restless. She's crying for Mama. I thought you'd want to know...' The last chords had only just faded as the young Spanish nurserymaid stood uncomfortably in the doorway, her worried gaze fastened on her employer. 'I've tried to comfort her, but...'

'Of course, Conchita, I'll come immediately.' Instantly Pavane rose from the piano stool. 'You'll all forgive me, won't you? She's having some trouble cutting a tooth at the moment and it makes her a little fractious. We've got a gel to rub on, but it doesn't always work, and a kiss and a cuddle will do wonders!'

'A universal panacea for a great number of ills,' Rico remarked drily as his sister-in-law followed Conchita from the room.

'But not always so instantly available on demand!' Esteban rose a trifle unsteadily to his feet and advanced towards the decanter of brandy on the nearby table. 'You permit, *amigo*?'

'*Por cierto*—what is mine is yours, *amigo*.' A lazy wave of Rico's hand invited Esteban to help himself, as the sudden high-pitched beep of a telephone broke into the warm stillness of the night.

Rico hauled himself to his feet with a sigh. 'Probably my brother, unable to settle down for the night without assuring himself of the safety and happiness of his dependants.' Mockery tinged his comment. 'I'd better put his mind at rest.'

'Lucky Armando!' Esteban's voice was thick with alcohol and something more which might have been misery, as Rico left the room. 'Not many marriages are as ideal as his!' To Merle's consternation he drained the remainder of his drink and rose to refill his glass.

It was none of her business, but something was very wrong with Rico's friend and, whatever the problem, his unrestricted intake of alcohol wasn't going to mitigate it, that was for sure!

'It must be difficult being separated from your wife so soon after your marriage,' she hazarded experimentally. 'But I expect she'll soon be here, won't she?'

'Huh!' Esteban sat down heavily beside her, placing his refilled glass on the table, much to her relief, rather than sampling its contents. 'The truth of the matter is that Isadora has left me, abandoned me. She refuses to speak to me, let alone come here to meet my parents and friends. She says it's all over between us.'

'Oh!' Merle felt totally out of her depth. Obviously Esteban needed counselling, and urgently, but not from her. Such a job needed qualifications she certainly didn't possess.

'What should I do?' Clearly Esteban didn't share her opinion of her capabilities as he turned pleading eyes on her startled face. 'Perhaps you can tell me what's gone wrong? You're both about the same age and probably share the same outlook on life. She's very independent and sure of herself, but she's been putting off meeting my parents, and now she's chosen to visit her friend rather than join me here.' His voice deepened to a growl. 'Yesterday I phoned her and ordered her to come here immediately if she wanted to remain my wife...'

'And she said she didn't?' Merle asked softly as he nodded glumly.

'I've phoned her since and she refuses to speak to me. She just left a message saying it was all over between us. *Dios*, Merle, what the hell do I do now?'

'Go and see her?' she suggested gently.

'Crawl, you mean?' All the arrogance of Andalusia sharpened his tone as Merle suppressed a smile.

'Actually all I meant was talk to her face to face. Had you considered she might be afraid of meeting your parents? After all, they were excluded from the wedding, and, independent though she may be in her job, you told me earlier today that she had no close family ties herself. It may be much more of an ordeal for her than you can possibly imagine.'

'Mmm.' He didn't look particularly convinced, but at least he was turning the idea over in his mind.

'Ordering her back would only have aggravated the situation,' Merle continued quickly, warming to her theme. 'She may feel she can never make you understand. If I'm right she needs your support, not your condemnation.'

'So what should I say?' If it hadn't been so serious for Esteban, Merle would have seen the funny side of the situation, but she was too sensitive to allow even the glimmer of a smile to touch her eyes as she met his anxious gaze.

'Just that you love her, I guess,' she told him simply. 'And that you're so proud of her that you can't wait to show her off to your family, who will be bound to care for her as much as you do...and...and that you've come over to escort her back home and give her all the loving support she needs.'

For a few moments Esteban stared back at her silently before leaning forward to take her hands in his own. 'Do you really think that will do it?'

He was bemused by brandy and showing an indecision Merle was sure he would regret when he sobered up, but she had taken on the burden of advising him, however foolhardily, and she was bound to follow it through. Even if she had misread the situation surely no harm could be done by Esteban telling his wife he loved her? At least it would get them on speaking terms again. It was entirely possible that Isadora was just as miserable as her estranged husband. Merle had no doubt but that it had been a love match originally, and the odds must be in favour of a reconciliation if the two protagonists could meet.

'I think it's the only thing you *can* do,' she told him honestly, adding for good measure, 'Remember it takes a strong man to make the first move, and Isadora will appreciate that, I'm sure.'

'Yes, I think you're right.' The dark eyes filled with warmth as his hands tightened around hers. 'I think you're marvellous Merle, so...so...*perspicaz*!'

He was gazing avidly into her earnest face when Rico re-entered the room, his countenance hard and unsmiling.

'That was the clinic,' he said without preamble. 'There's been a bad accident on the Cordoba road and they're transferring a patient to the clinic tomorrow morning for treatment.' His stern gaze flickered over Merle to rest on Esteban. 'I'm sure you'll understand that I need a good night's sleep in the circumstances, so if you're ready, I'll drive you back to the hacienda.' His appraisal was scathing as it lingered on his friend's flushed face. 'For certain you're in no fit state to drive yourself in the Jeep. One unexpected operation to re-build a human body is enough to be going on with!'

'Oh, Esteban can stay here.' Pavane came in hurriedly, having overheard Rico's last speech. 'There's always a spare room ready...'

'Thank you, but I think I'd better go back.' Esteban pulled himself to his feet. 'I can't begin to tell you how much I've enjoyed the evening...'

'Good, then we'll be going!' Curtly Rico truncated the other man's appreciation and led the way from the *sala* with an urgent stride.

Pavane made a little gesture of despair as they heard the front door close behind the two men. 'It's probably a child who's been injured. Rico's too professional to be a prey to emotion usually—it's just sometimes that it gets to him.'

Merle nodded understandingly, refusing her hostess's next offer of more coffee or a further drink and stating her own intention of going to bed.

It had been a strange evening, she brooded several minutes later, stepping out of the shower and patting herself dry. Rico had behaved with impeccable manners until that last moment, when he had seemed to lose the patina of politeness to reveal a more basic side to his nature.

Merle reached for the aerosol container which con-tained the matching body foam to her favourite perfume and began to massage the creamy mixture into her warm skin, inhaling pleasurably the delicate aroma it released. Rico had almost kicked Esteban out, and it wasn't even as if it had been his own house. Correctly speaking, as

Pavane was mistress of the house, Esteban had been her guest . . .

The tap at the door, which could only be Pavane—for who else was there to disturb her at this hour?—interrupted her musings. Hastily donning her pink satin nightshirt, she didn't bother to button its neck as her skin still glowed from the warmth of the shower and the lingering warmth of the Andalusian night.

'Come in—I was just having a shower . . .' The words stilled in her throat as she opened the door and found herself facing Rico. Without conscious volition her fingers tightened their grasp on the polished olivewood knob of the door. 'I thought you were Pavane,' she accused, flushing involuntarily and praying he would attribute her risen colour to the warmth of the shower rather than to his own unexpected appearance.

Unprepared for him to accept the invitation she had meant for Pavane, she stepped back, shocked, as he crossed the threshold, closing the door behind him and leaning against it while his dark eyes swept over her.

'Leave Esteban alone, Merle. He's a married man.'

'What?' A tremor of fear mingled with the horror that drained the blood from her face.

'You heard me.' His quiet tone was more alarming than if he had shouted at her, robbing her of words. 'He's vulnerable because Isadora's away and he's missing her badly, but he doesn't need you as a substitute, however willing you are to console him. Do you understand what I'm saying?'

'I *hear* you.' Her voice was shaking so badly she had to pause and gather herself together before continuing. 'But I don't *understand* you. There's nothing between your friend and me.'

'And there isn't going to be.' His brilliant gaze pinned her, intimate, deliberately caustic. 'I won't let you make the same mistakes I did. There can never be any joy in coming between two people who love each other—and Esteban's marriage deserves a chance, whatever the reason for Isadora's prolonged absence—and however overheated our Spanish climate has made your cool Gaelic blood.'

'Get out of my room!' If Rico had slapped her round the face Merle couldn't have felt more hurt and humiliated. She wouldn't stoop to defending herself—not that he would have believed her if she'd told him the truth!

'Not before I have your undertaking to keep your distance.' He moved towards her, every inch of his body threatening as she backed further away, determined not to surrender to his absurd demand. 'How do you think I felt when I came back from answering the phone and found you gazing into each other's eyes, your fingers entwined?' He gave a brief sarcastic bark of laughter. 'When I told Esteban that what was mine was also his, I was being polite.' His beautiful white teeth showed briefly as his lips curled sneeringly. 'I hardly expected him to take me at my word where you were concerned, but I might have guessed he wouldn't be able to resist the invitation to drown in your beautiful eyes!'

'I was never yours!' Merle seized on the most hurtful point, her accusing eyes mirroring her intensity, her fast shallow breathing a witness to her agitation.

'That could so easily be remedied.' Rico's contemplative gaze travelled slowly over her body, making her horribly aware of the shortness of the pink satin which clung damply to her tense breasts, the length of naked leg revealed to his encompassing stare. She felt her whole body glow with an inner heat as his words burned into her brain.

'You know my terms!' Pride lent her the courage to taunt him, but his quick aggressive movement towards

her had her stepping backwards once again, only to catch
her calf against the soft edge of the chaise-longue, and
to be forced to sit down abruptly on its velvet softness.

'And what was Esteban prepared to pay for the privi-
lege of taking you to bed, eh, *dulzura mia*?' Firm hands
reached to grasp her wrists in an implacable hold as he
dragged her to her feet. Only inches divided them as he
glowered down at her. 'Or was the challenge of taking
another woman's husband satisfaction enough for you?'

Goose-pimples caused by the scorn in his voice rose
on the exposed skin of her upper arms, while her pulse
beat in a wild rhythm to augment the gathering heat of
her temper. 'Who better than you to answer a question
like that?' Bitterly angry, she returned his furious stare,
delighted when her retort had his breath hissing in as if
he had been stung.

Every cell in her body was vibrating as its warmth liberated the exotic aura of her perfume to surround them.
Fear? No. Although she half expected Rico to punish
her, if not with the flat of his hand, then with the angry
contemptuous pressure of his mouth against her own,
the emotion building in her was a tumultuous sense of
expectation and excitement rather than terror, a force
that was spiralling to a vortex in which anything would
be possible.

With a sick sense of shock Merle recognised that her
body was immune to the insults being levelled at her ego
and that if Rico took her in his arms at that moment
she would be like putty in his hands, moulding herself
to the strong lines of his body and accepting any pleasure
or punishment he thought fit to administer with a deep
resignation to the inevitable.

Never in her life had every nerve in her body screamed
in a torment born of injustice and a wild physical attraction that answered to no logic.

Painfully aware of the heightened tension of her breasts beneath their satin covering, the ache of her engorged nipples against the soft rub of material, and the yawning need streaming through her being, she could do nothing but watch the strange mingling of hauteur and pain on Rico's dark countenance.

'*Es verdad...*' He spoke softly, with none of the overt fury she had anticipated, yet she could feel the sheer force of his personality reaching out to her, weakening her justifiable bitterness. 'Which is why I don't intend for you to abuse my brother's hospitality while you are living under his roof.'

'And you don't consider you're doing just that by forcing yourself into my room and maligning me?' Try as she might she couldn't prevent her breath catching in a half-sob in her throat.

'You invited me in, Merle,' he told her quietly, only the muscle that twitched beneath his cheekbone betraying his calmness as being the result of iron self-control rather than indifference. 'Believe me, I'm well aware of the obligations of hospitality... besides...' his smile was cruel rather than humorous '...it's not in my nature to take anything unless it's freely offered,' again a tiny pause before he added, 'or it's been bought and paid for. Look at me!'

The last instruction was rapped out with such power that Merle responded obediently, raising eyes that had momentarily strayed, to focus on his face. Silently absorbing the beautiful bones, the strongly rounded chin with its dark shadow advertising both his heritage and the lateness of the hour, the sweet curve of his mouth now hardened to a line of condemnation, she waited for him to speak again.

'Stay away from Esteban, or you'll live to regret it.'

'You dare to threaten me?' Some last remnant of pride forced her to challenge him as he released her wrists, her eyes flashing a sapphire fire as she lifted her chin haughtily.

'Only to warn you. We have a proverb in Spain: "Take what you want," said God. "Take what you want—and pay for it." The point being that invariably the price is more than the desire is worth, and believe me—Esteban is not for you.'

He turned abruptly, leaving the room without a backward glance, closing the door firmly behind him, abandoning her shaken and trembling to face the lonely hours of the night before sleep claimed her, shamed by his baseless accusation and mortified by the knowledge that, although only her wrists had known his touch, every cell of her body had responded to the latent power of his arrant masculinity with an abandonment which had been entirely beyond her conscious control.

CHAPTER TEN

ARRIVING at breakfast the following morning to find only Pavane, Nacio and Elena present, Merle felt absolute relief.

'Rico left first thing this morning,' her hostess told her, offering a basket of warm croissants across the table. 'He never discusses the work he does, but I can't help feeling he's concerned about the outcome of this particular operation. He's not usually so taciturn, and he did say not to expect him back for a couple of nights. I do hope his absence won't spoil your stay too much.'

'No, not at all,' Merle hastened to assure her valiantly, wondering how Pavane would react if she knew just how pleased her unexpected guest was to be deserted by her apparent patron. In fact she had spent a good part of the previous night frustrated beyond belief because Barbie's proposed visit had effectively prevented her from pleading a need to see Laurie again as an excuse to return immediately to England and leave Rico to savour his nasty suspicions in isolation!

'I'm sure we can keep you amused,' Pavane was continuing cheerfully. 'Nacio wants to show you how well he can swim and Elena wants you to see her doll's house.' She cast a loving eye on her two offspring, intent on enjoying their breakfasts. 'And to be honest, I could do with some help in planning the menu for Sunday's party! Ana, our housekeeper, will be organising all the catering once I've decided on a buffet menu, but I'd like to do something a little different. Do you know, I haven't seen my brother-in-law Ramón since my wedding day over nine years ago! And Pablo, his son, must be eighteen now...' Her eyes sparkled with laughter. 'I looked after Pablo for a short while after I was first married and before he joined his parents in Brazil, and I must admit I can't wait to see what he looks like now. Even at nine he had all the embryo qualities of looks and charm that make the Montilla men so compelling.'

'Rico...' Even his name on her tongue was difficult for Merle to handle without betraying herself. 'Rico is certainly compelling—perhaps overpowering would be a better description!' Despite her efforts the comment lacked the light-heartedness she had hoped to convey, drawing towards herself a sharp look from Pavane.

'As a matter of fact Rico is a very compassionate man, much more vulnerable than most people would ever guess. Not that he'd thank me for telling you! I'm afraid he sets himself impossibly high standards and is his own severest judge when he fails to meet the criterion he has set out to attain. If he were less harsh with himself I'm sure he'd get more pleasure out of life...' Pavane sighed. 'But enough of the Montillas—you'll have your fill of them on Sunday! In the meantime we've got to arrange a programme for you so that you get the best out of the coming days.'

Breakfast passed pleasantly as Pavane chattered on happily, telling Merle about her early girlhood in England and how her great-aunt's death had brought her to Spain to stay with her sister Melody, who had already married a Spanish landowner. Without prying she encouraged Merle to confide some of her earlier life. Merle kept the information she divulged light and general, feeling under no pressure. More and more she was finding herself drawn to the pretty blonde who had offered her such a warm welcome.

Certainly the day flew past, divided between swimming and sunbathing and playing with the children in the morning and a tour of the outer regions of the estate in the afternoon, undertaken in a Jeep driven by the farm manager.

By the time evening came Merle was feeling much more relaxed, her skin warmly blushed from careful exposure to the sun, her spirits high because Barbie had phoned to say their flight was booked for Sunday and they would be arriving at Seville at six in the evening after a short stop-over at Barcelona. The older girl had greeted the idea of the party with great enthusiasm, declaring herself thrilled to be able to participate in a real piece of Spanish life and promising to pack her best party dress for the occasion.

At least, Merle thought, brushing her hair with thoughtful strokes that night, Rico's absence had given her time to breathe and recollect her senses, and to remind herself that whatever she felt for him there wasn't a snowball's chance in hell of the attractive Andalusian ever forgiving her for what he saw as a wilful deception—whatever other feelings he might harbour towards her.

Tomorrow, Friday, Pavane had suggested a trip into Seville, something Merle was really looking forward to, especially since her last visit had been so full of unresolved trauma. This time she determined she would relax and enjoy the experience. Perhaps she'd even lash out on a new dress for Sunday's celebration!

In all probability it would be the last day she would ever set eyes on Rico de Montilla. Some perverse pride dictated that she should go out of his life in style. He had set himself up as a knight on a white charger for motives she couldn't begin to analyse, but such figures belonged to fairy-tales. The reality was that she had lost

Paraiso for all time, and with it any hope of time re-kindling the camaraderie she had once shared with him. It was the last thought she had before falling to sleep.

True to her expectations, the following day's shopping expedition proved a great success, Pavane clapping her hands in unrestrained approval as Merle paraded in the dress she had seen in a boutique and fallen in love with. In royal-blue georgette with a low-scooped neck and long filmy sleeves, it had a full swirling skirt beneath a nipped-in waist which emphasised her curvaceous figure, moving seductively against her calves as she twisted around for her companion's benefit.

It was late afternoon before the two girls returned to the *cortijo*, having enjoyed a leisurely meal in one of the delightful outdoor restaurants, and Merle was content to spend the rest of the day at leisure in the grounds of the estate.

The following morning she sang softly to herself as she stepped from the shower. Tomorrow she would see Laurie again and be freed from the oppressive power of the man whose presence in her life earlier on was causing her such anguish. Rico... Resolutely she forced her mind away from him, telling herself that hungering after forbidden fruit had been the cause of Eve's downfall. It wasn't a precedent she wanted to follow!

Thoughtfully she selected tiny cotton briefs and a strapless bra to wear: the latter kinder to her sun-kissed shoulders. Even though it was so early in the season the day promised to be another scorcher, she determined, reaching for the pretty print skirt she had worn on her first visit to Seville. The matching bolero neatly covered the bra, tying loosely just above her waist so that the fresh air could circulate freely against her warm skin.

Hadn't Pavane said something about their going down to Jazmin to make sure that everything was in order before Barbie and Co arrived tomorrow? Thrusting her feet into her favourite wedge-heeled sandals, Merle gave herself one last cursory look in the mirror, twisting her hair into a loose knot on top of her head and securing it with hairgrips masked with a small white chiffon bow.

'*Buenos días!*' Delighted with the progress she had been making under Pavane's willing tuition, she uttered her usual morning greeting as she stepped out on to the patio.

'*Buenos días*, Merle.' There was no mistaking the leanly elegant figure that rose to greet her from his place at the table.

'Oh, you're back!' It was an inane remark as Merle felt a slow tide of colour flow into her cheeks. For some reason she had imagined he would stay in Cadiz until tomorrow's party.

'Evidently.' His amused glance fed on her discomfort. 'And none too welcome, by appearances.'

'I—I . . .' As quickly as it had come the colour ebbed from her face. Goodness knew what feelings she was betraying to the discerning eye of the man whose gaze concentrated on her. To think she'd almost persuaded herself she had become immune to him in his absence! With the blood hammering in her veins and a hollow sickness silently torturing her midriff, she admitted the enormity of her error. 'I just wasn't expecting to see you today,' she finished weakly, adding quickly, 'Was the operation successful?'

'Fortunately, yes.' Rico's quick smile was absolutely genuine, lending his saturnine face a wicked charm that made the breath catch in her throat. 'There was fear at first that we might have to amputate. Fortunately that has been avoided. There will be scars . . .' he shrugged

'...but we hope not too unsightly, and the main thing is that mobility should be nearly a hundred per cent in time.' He pulled out a chair. 'Won't you join me, Merle? Pavane and the children had breakfast early this morning. My sister-in-law's busy discussing tomorrow with Ana, and the children are in the nursery ensuring that Conchita earns her wages.'

'Thank you—*gracias*!' Her resolve was paying off as her confidence began to return, nourished by the growing realisation that Rico appeared to have forgotten the way they had parted. If he was going to play the perfect host for the rest of the day it was just possible she would be able to relax, even begin to enjoy his company as she had in those far-off days, she thought wistfully, wondering which would cause her most pain—Rico unjustifiably furious or Rico unexpectedly tender.

Breakfast was always the same: rolls and croissants, butter, black cherry jam or Pavane's home-made Sevillan marmalade which Rico assured her with unstinted admiration had become something of a cult among the estate workers. Coffee was supplied in an enormous silver coffee-pot with tea available on request.

With a small dip of her head acknowledging his invitation, Merle seated herself, accepting a roll and spreading it with the delicious tart marmalade provided.

'Coffee?' Rico barely waited for her nod of acquiescence before filling her cup. 'Pavane's asked me to apologise to you, but there's been some drama in the kitchen—nothing serious, but something which demands her attention——' A lofty hand waved away his interest in further details of a domestic problem. 'But it seems she won't be able to drive over to the coast with you to make sure everything in the villa's up to standard, so I've offered my services instead.'

'That's very kind of you.' Even to her own ears the words seemed cold and formal. Rather that than he should guess how her heart seemed to do acrobatics at the very thought of an enforced journey in his company.

'De nada.' He matched her politeness, very Latin in his rebuttal of her gratitude.

Too conscious of his eyes resting on her every action, Merle felt her hand shake as she offered a small piece of roll to her mouth, feeling his penetrating gaze watching every movement of her lips as she swallowed the mouthful and washed it down with a long draught of coffee.

'I've one or two things to do before we leave, so I thought we'd aim to arrive at the villa in time to take an inventory and then have lunch there—I understand there's plenty of food laid in. The main things we need to check are cutlery and crockery, and of course you'll be able to tell me if there's anything missing that your sister would require. That way we can arrange for the deficiencies to be made good first thing Monday morning before she takes possession.'

Merle abandoned the remains of her roll, pushing her plate away, too unnerved by Rico's steady appraisal to continue eating. 'I don't know why you're doing all this for me,' she told him honestly.

'Don't you?' His smile was enigmatic, his eyes behind the dark flare of lashes echoing the amusement in his voice. 'Let's just say, for the time being, that it's because of what might have been. Does that satisfy you?

Fortunately he didn't wait for her answer, because she had none to give him. Instead he rose lazily to his feet. 'I'll be ready to leave in about two hours.'

Watching his departure, her gaze feasting on the breadth of his shoulders beneath the thin cambric shirt, drifting downwards to encompass the line of his leather belt above the hip-hugging Levis that emphasised his muscular leanness, Merle felt her mouth go dry. How bitter the pain to long so avidly for his favour when she had forfeited it so completely from the moment she had cast her first tremulous, innocent smile on his compelling features.

In fact it was about fifteen minutes short of two hours when Rico sought her out to enquire if she was ready to depart.

'Of course.' Merle rose to her feet and accompanied him to where the car waited for them. 'I do hope that having to do this isn't interfering with any other plans you might have made.' She slid gracefully into the passenger seat as he closed the door behind her.

'Not at all.' He was all suave politeness as he took his seat beside her and turned the key in the ignition. 'As a matter of fact, I can't think of a more pleasant way of spending the day.'

She cast a quick suspicious look at the strong profile presented to her. No, there was no suspicion of sarcasm marring its classic lines. Had he come to the conclusion that he had misjudged her intentions towards Esteban? Or perhaps he had ascertained from Pavane that Enrico's son had been nowhere near the *cortijo* during his absence. If that was the case she would very much like to receive her short-tempered host's humble apology. An expression of contrition would sit strangely on Rico's arrogant features and would have given her much pleasure! Unfortunately, to demand it might necessitate her relating Esteban's confidences, and that would be unforgivable.

On the other hand, Rico's observation probably applied to the prospect of going down to the coast rather than spending the time in her company. At least it appeared he wasn't going to be boringly disparaging, and that was something for which Merle was extremely grateful. She had greeted his announcement at breakfast with some trepidation. Now it seemed it had been un-merited. The day might prove to be enjoyable after all.

The sun was high in the sky when the Seat turned into the road leading to the Villa Jazmin—and continued right past it.

'Where are we going?' Surprised, even wondering if Rico had been thinking of other things, Merle half turned in her seat towards him, eyebrows raised enquiringly.

'I thought we'd take a look at the Villa Paraiso.' A few hundred yards further on he parked the Seat off the road. 'Make sure that no one's vandalised it.'

'Oh, surely they wouldn't!' she protested, never-theless obeying his unspoken command and alighting into the shimmering heat of mid-morning, not at all sure that she wanted to set eyes on the villa again. 'Must we?'

Rico shrugged indifferently, winding up the windows of the car before locking the door. 'It won't do any harm to have a look and it'll do us good to stretch our legs and feel the wind on our faces.'

Well, that was reasonable enough, Merle concurred, stretching her limbs with a feline grace and enjoying the caress of the salt-laden Atlantic breeze as it played with the escaped tendrils of dark hair that curled round her face, as she prepared to follow in Rico's footsteps.

'Oh, no!' Minutes later a wounded cry of protest burst from her lips. She had prepared herself for seeing her dream home turned into an impregnable fortress—but the reality was far worse. Gone were the chains and no-tices, the bars at the windows and the spiked gates barring access to the upper storey. The white stone gleamed, the natural wood shutters were immaculate against their purity, the revealed windows shielded by internal blinds. Flowers tumbled down in brilliant array from the first-floor balcony and she could see the top of a dark blue sun-umbrella fringed with white flexing as the light wind caught it.

All the time she had known she was fighting a useless battle. She had no reason to feel so totally devastated, but disappointment struck her like a blow to her stomach so that she had to swallow several times in quick succession to relieve the wave of nausea she experienced.

'He's already sold it!' She turned anguished eyes to Rico, making a valiant effort to hold back the tears that were already too near the surface.

He couldn't have heard her, because after casting an appraising look over the villa he opened the gates and strolled into the garden.

'Rico, we can't!' Hurriedly she moved after him, catching him by the arm as he reached the front door. 'It's too late to do anything now. Obviously your lawyer was unsuccessful. It's already been sold to someone else!'

'It's possible.' Rico turned to face her, lifting her hand from his arm, searching her troubled face with every sign of compassion. 'On the other hand, Merlita...' he thrust his right hand deep into the pocket of his Levis '...it may have been restored to its rightful owner.'

She stood stock-still, unable to believe what she saw as Rico produced a key, fitted it with leisurely ease into the lock and opened the door.

'Welcome home, Merle.'

'I don't understand...' Was this some kind of obscene joke at her expense? No—instinctively she knew Rico would never stoop to such cruelty, but still her eyes pleaded for reassurance as she fought down the swelling knot of excitement which threatened to disrupt her nervous system, in case it should prove premature.

'What more is there to understand?' His smile flipped her heart. 'I told you Fidelio Diaz was a man of many parts and that human nature has more virtue in it than most people suspect. It seems our Señor Sanchez had no wish to steal the widow's mite when the facts were explained to him. He agreed to accept the settlement of the debt plus the accrued interest.'

'How long have you known?' No longer could Merle contain the joy she felt as, half laughing, half crying, she crossed the threshold.

'Since yesterday morning,' Rico acknowledged, closing the door behind them. 'I hope you'll forgive the liberty I took, but I wanted you to see your Paraiso in the best possible light. I arranged for it to be cleaned and prepared for you.'

'Oh, Rico!' The eyes she turned on him were swimming with tears. 'I can't believe it! You must have had an army of people working on it!'

'Quite a few,' he agreed equably. 'The name of Montilla y Cabra carries a lot of weight in this part of the world—a benefit for which my brother deserves full credit.'

He was being unduly modest, she was sure, as she sped from room to room, delightedly surveying everything that had been accomplished, her elation increasing with each perfect revelation.

'I thought we'd eat on the balcony,' Rico smiled at her flushed face, the enthusiasm she wouldn't have hidden from him even if she'd been able to do so. 'Everything should have been provided to order, so by the time you've checked upstairs, luncheon will be served.'

'Yes, fine!' Delightedly Merle ran up the open-plan staircase. Here again everything sparkled. Three bedrooms, each with a double bed made up for use, a large bathroom with shining tiles complete with lemon verbena soap and thick fluffy towels that matched the pale lemon walls... Catching sight of her face in the mirror, Merle raised her palms to its warm surface. She was almost drunk with pleasure—the adrenalin flowing through her veins lifting her to a state bordering on ecstasy. Calm down! she apostrophised herself, thrilled when the cold tap duly delivered clear cool water. Splashing it on her face, she tried to get her elation under control. Rico deserved someone better than a half-crazed woman as a companion for his meal!

It was in a more composed state of mind that she eventually walked through the door at the end of the first-floor corridor leading to the balcony, to find the table laid and a bottle of champagne nestled in an ice bucket awaiting her arrival.

'Well?' Rico rose to greet her. 'Is everything satisfactory?'

She swallowed in an attempt to keep her voice steady. 'I don't know how I'll ever be able to thank you...'

'No?' With the unerring courtesy he had always showed at the table Rico pulled out a soft-cushioned chair for her to sit down upon. 'Surely you haven't forgotten our arrangement?'

For a micro-second she didn't understand him, and then realisation burst upon her with shattering effect. She had been too overjoyed to remember what she had said to him. Now the words came back to her, echoing with an appalling clarity—'I'm quite happy for us to become lovers...the day you give me the key to Paraiso.'

'I hope the menu pleases you.' Rico, having delivered his bombshell, was continuing the conversation as if nothing had changed. 'The first course is honey-glazed quail, followed by scampi cacciatore and a side salad with lemon sorbet to clear the palate before profiteroles and cream, with champagne, of course, to ease its passage.'

He didn't seem to expect an answer, which was just as well, because what could she say? She had made a statement and, unlikely though it had been that she would be called on to honour it, she had known then—as she did now—that she would; and although the knowledge shamed her she admitted to herself that it would not be under duress.

'A truly international menu, I believe.' The muscle in Rico's arms tensed as he thumbed the champagne cork, sending it exploding into the air. 'To the repossession of Paraiso...' He filled her glass, indicating that she join him in the toast.

'To Paraiso,' she murmured faintly, swallowing the liquid sparkle with more enthusiasm than good sense. 'You must let me know how much I owe you, plus Señor Diaz's fee, of course.'

'Call it a house-warming present.' Neatly Rico uncovered the foil-wrapped dishes, exposing the golden-brown quail garnished with shredded salad.

'Oh, no! I couldn't possibly do that!' Horror made her voice rise. 'The cost must be several thousand pesetas, and I can well afford it!'

'So can I.' There was no laughter now on the beautiful male face which dared her to contest his will. 'And since it's Fidelio Diaz who has done all the work and I who will reap the benefits of his endeavour I feel it's the very least I can do. More champagne?'

Her glass was empty, and she lacked the bravura to prevent his filling it to the brim. She could have expected no more, yet to find herself treated as a woman who sold her favours was the most humiliating ordeal she had ever faced in her life. Presumably Rico was used to such encounters, for he seemed totally unperturbed by her sudden lapse into silence.

Merle ate like an automaton as one delicious course followed another, allowing Rico to pour her one further glass of champagne. She wasn't going to make the situation worse by being too inebriated to know what she was doing. Suppose she reneged on her bargain? Told Rico it had been a spur-of-the-moment retort never intended seriously? No, that was impossible. Her pride was equal to his any day, and she would never have made the offer if it had gone totally against the grain. That was the hardest part to admit to herself: that she *wanted* Rico as a lover, that she wanted the one last glorious memory of him held in her arms...

'Shall we?' Panic caught at her throat as she realised she could prolong the duration of the meal no longer, the dregs of her second cup of black coffee grown cold in the cup.

Stiffly she rose to her feet, allowing Rico to propel her gently into the comparative dimness of the villa. At the door of the main bedroom she hesitated.

'Rico, I...'

'Yes?' He was patience personified, courteously waiting for her to continue. The embryo protest died on her tongue. If he had been impatient or even excessively ardent she might have been able to dredge up the indignation she needed to repulse him. This quiet businesslike manner defeated her utterly. 'Nothing,' she whispered.

'Ah, Merle...' He took her hand, drawing her towards the bed, sitting down on it and pulling her on to his lap. *'Mi mujer bella...'* Suddenly he was no longer the cool, slightly superior man whose indifference had taunted her for the past hour, as one hand slid beneath her bolero to discover and remove with indolent ease the simple bra it discovered. As his fingers forked beneath her swelling breasts, raising them to his lips, and he bent his ebony

head the better to caress their tumid apexes, Merle felt
her mind spin in helpless agony, her body blossoming
into a hitherto unknown arousal, passion surging like a
storm through every cell of her being.

With a moan, half pain, half pleasure she lifted her
hand to latch her fingers through the dark glory of his
hair, burying her face in its softness as the rising golden
tide of ecstasy coursing through her veins demanded.

At last his soft warm mouth left her flesh as he eased
himself a few inches away, his voice hoarse, to stare down
into her flushed face, her wide blue eyes luminous with
emotion. 'I'm not going to release you from your
promise... If that's what you're waiting for, Merlita,
then it's not going to happen...unless...'
He heaved in a deep breath and his hands tightened
around her while she stared back into his grim face, her
lips parted in unconscious invitation. 'Unless,' he continued harshly, 'you tell me you've had a change of heart.
No explanations necessary—just one word. Just "no",
Merle, and we'll leave now—get into the car and drive
back to the *cortijo*...'

Suddenly he was the man she had met on the beach,
compassionate, caring and tender, and her heart swelled
with the love which had always lain dormant there.

'No...' She would deny him nothing—no, that wasn't
right, she would deny *them* nothing. With a certainty
she knew it was her destiny to be joined with this man,
however brief the union, however transient the joy; it
had been written in her stars.

When Rico eased her off his lap and rose to his feet
she turned towards him with starry eyes, eager for him
to lead her into unknown pleasure, certain he was about
to help her discard the few items of clothing that kept
her hidden from his gaze. It was several painful seconds,
during which she saw but didn't comprehend the stark

tautness of his face and discerned the way his fingers trembled as he smoothed down his shirt as if fighting to regain control over himself, before she realised he had misunderstood her sharp ejaculation.

'Rico!' She was off the bed, flinging her arms around him, totally unselfconscious in her need to reassure him, her heart thumping painfully as she felt his whole body tense against her. 'I meant—no, I haven't had a change of heart!'

'Are you sure?' The words were torn out of him, then as she nodded he found her mouth with a passion and purpose that had her gasping as he swept her up into his arms.

'I've dreamed of this for so long...' He laid her gently on the bed, and his words were as gentle as the soft caressing movements of his able hands as he paid homage to her beauty, untying and discarding the light bolero, fondling her pale breasts with sensitive fingers, deliberately controlling his own urgency to incite a wondrous pleasure that sent sensuous shivers trembling up and down her spine, as he murmured soft endearments in his native tongue with a thrilling huskiness.

Merle was quivering with anticipation before he left her side to strip off the few garments which clothed his own magnificent body. In the stillness of the room shadowed by half-closed shutters she watched his powerful silhouette, feeling a poignant stab of longing as her eyes dwelt on the raised weals that decorated the satin smoothness of his back.

If he had rushed it, the experience could never have been so good, so satisfying for her. Even as her body shed the sweet musky tears of love Merle's heart leapt with joy at the solicitude shown by the strong man who had both captured and become her captive.

Rico loved her with infinite forbearance, marvellously aware of her desires and doubts. She wanted nothing from him but the satisfaction of knowing she had been the instrument of his pleasure. It wasn't the thought of a liberated woman, just an instinctive emotion which she need never publicly acknowledge or apologise for; but he gave her so much more than that, wreaking an awesome magic on her untutored body, until in her need she whimpered for release, lifting her hips to receive him and hold him completely and tightly with an expertise which owed nothing to experience and everything to instinct and the love she bore him.

There was no pain or discomfort as she had half feared. Nothing to detract from the glory of taking him and finding herself possessed by him in a mutual agony of sensation. Belonging to him in that fierce act of dominion where power always replaced persuasion, Merle moved with and against Rico's vital male body in perfect harmony until the pleasure became too intense to contain, spiralling into a plane of ecstasy before stilling into a shining peace.

All her life she would remember this afternoon, the harsh beauty of Rico's face, the dark ebony of his hair on the pale cover, the slumbrous heavily lashed eyes closing as his sharp cry of exultation pierced the silence and she felt his weight grow heavy on her for a few seconds before he rolled away.

Carefully, quietly, she swung her legs off the bed, gathering her clothes together before making her way to the en-suite bathroom. It wasn't unusual for a man to sleep in such circumstances, she knew. Methodically she showered, re-dressed and brushed out her hair, which had become impossibly tumbled. When she re-entered the bedroom Rico was still stretched out on his face, his sable head buried into the pillow, the lean muscularity of his virile body simply stunning.

Quite unable to resist the temptation, Merle approached the bed, bending to place her lips, as soft as the touch of the breeze, in swift salutation on the raised tissue of his back which evidenced his resolve and his bravery.

Briskly she collected her senses, walking out on to the balcony to clear the table. Downstairs she filled the sink with warm water, delighted at the efficiency of the solar panels in the roof and, finding some liquid in the cupboard, began to wash up.

Filled with a quiet satisfaction, she was aware that nothing would ever be quite the same again after what had occurred between Rico and herself. She felt stronger for the experience—as if she had taken some of his power. He had imprinted his body on her, and although the physical sensation of his possession, which still lingered, would fade, the memory of his power and purpose would live with her forever, sustaining her.

CHAPTER ELEVEN

MERLE was smiling to herself as she turned her attention to the task in hand. She had been too caught up in events before to examine the plates and glasses. Now she realised she was handling the finest porcelain and lead crystal. Carefully she rinsed and dried them. These were certainly not part of Paraiso's inventory!

A sound behind her made her turn as Rico entered the room, fully dressed and groomed to perfection.

One thing she did know. It wasn't the done thing to hold a post-mortem after a casual relationship. The smart thing was to ignore what had happened, relegating it to 'just one of those things' rather than an event which had revolutionised her life.

'Hi,' she greeted him cheerfully. 'You're just too late to dry for me. Did you provide the china and glass from Jazmin—it certainly didn't come with the fittings!'

'Yes, they're mine.' Rico moved forward to lift a glass, holding it towards the window so that the sun reflected baubles of light from it to dance across the ceiling. 'I supplied them as well as the food and wine—everything was identical with the plans I made last year when I went to your hotel to invite you to have dinner with me.'

A quick glance at his profile, eyes narrowed as he observed the glinting crystal in his hand, told her nothing—but there had been something in his tone which was curiously disturbing.

'Oh, you mean when you were going to ask me to become your lover?' she asked lightly.

'When I intended to ask you to be my wife.' The glass was abandoned on the table as he moved forward, removing the space between them to seize Merle by the shoulders.

'Wife?' Her voice cracked. 'But you said...'

'The only thing I could to protect my own pride! The truth was when we met it was *flechazo*, what you would call an arrow through the heart.'

'Love at first sight?' Unbelievably she saw him nod.

'You don't believe in it? Ah, Merle, it happens. Ask Armando—he saw Pavane across the aisle of a church and was lost. Nearly a decade later he is still entranced.' Rico smiled a little grimly. 'In the first few hours of meeting you I too was lost. I didn't need time. I knew everything I needed to know—it was written in your eyes, your voice, the way you walked, the way you smiled...'

Sensing what must follow, Merle took the initiative, uncertain where this conversation could possibly lead. 'Everything about me—except that I was married,' she whispered, looking away so that she didn't have to meet the accusation in his eyes.

'Yes...' It was almost a sigh as he released his grip to walk away from her, thrusting his hands deep into his pockets and staring moodily out of the window. 'It was like the end of the world—a judgement—a divine punishment, as if despite my contrition I still hadn't expiated my sins.'

'I'm sorry...' Merle's heart ached for him. If she had had any idea at all about the way he had felt...

'It wasn't your fault—I realise that now. It was my own wishful thinking that convinced my ego that you felt the same way about me. I mistook your natural compassion for a much deeper, more personal emotion; but at the time all I could think of was that you had deliberately used me for amusement. *Dios*, how that hurt!'

'Rico—I——' Merle licked lips grown unnaturally dry as adrenalin pumped through her veins in answer to the tension that simmered in the atmosphere between them.

He brushed aside her interruption, his voice harsh and deep. 'Then just when I thought I'd got you right out of my system you turned up on my doorstep and I knew I'd been fooling myself, that I would never be truly free of you. When I still believed you to be married I found the strength to fight my own weakness, but when you told me you were a widow... *Santa madre de Dios!* I kept telling myself that last year you'd been prepared to deceive your husband, deliberately alienating myself to avoid becoming involved with you again.'

Sadly Merle shook her head as he turned to face her, his features contorted with fervour. 'That was never true. I was reaching out for something, someone I needed, but I had no idea what I was doing! I can't explain in simple terms!' Her voice rose in anguish as she considered the complications of her life.

'Hush, *querida*, you don't have to.' Again she was in his arms, nestling her head against his chest as he soothed her. 'Eventually I had to face the facts. Without you my life would always lack meaning. I had to keep you here in Spain for as long as I could and try to persuade you to give me a chance to show how much I wanted you.' He sighed and she felt his whole body tremble with release. 'But you didn't want to know—and who could blame you after the way I treated you?—and then you offered yourself to me in exchange for the key to Paraiso and I dared to hope that once we had lain in each other's arms, touched intimately as man and woman, joined our bodies together in nature's most powerful union, you would give me the chance to share your life for more than one brief hour... give me the opportunity to prove how much I love you!'

Her heart clenching painfully as she fought down every instinct to agree to continuing their affair over the coming weeks, Merle raised one hand to touch Rico's cheek, feeling the muscle tighten beneath her fingertips. 'I—I can't. I have to think of Laurie. I can't consider any irregular relationship for her sake.' Wide-eyed, she begged his understanding.

'And marriage is irregular?' Rico pushed her gently away from him so that he could gaze quizzically into her astonished face. 'Nothing's changed, Merlita. I want you to be my wife. I want Laurie to be my daughter, to take her into my home and into my life, to give her the things her own father would have wanted for her. I want both of you, *mi corazón*. Is it such an impossible thing to ask? After what has just happened between us I dare to hope not.' His smile was heartbreakingly tender. 'I was lying on the bed a few minutes ago wondering if I stood any chance of ever winning your love—and then I felt your lips on my skin—and I dared to hope.' He paused for a long second. 'Was I wrong, Merle?'

For ten seconds Merle was silent, savouring the idea as if there was the slightest possibility of accepting it, and knowing it was totally impossible.

'Well?' he prompted her gently, forcing her out of her daydreams.

'There's something I have to tell you. Laurie's not my own child,' she said painfully. 'David was a fine man, but I never loved him. We never lived together as man and wife. I married him to give his daughter a stable home and preserve her inheritance...' She paused fearfully, as Rico exhaled his breath in a low hiss of shock.

'I didn't imagine it, then! I was the first man who has ever loved you!'

If the pain in her heart had been any less Merle would have laughed at his astounded face. 'I thought you hadn't realised.'

He shrugged, his expression still bemused. 'I thought it was so good, so incredibly perfect because I loved you so much, and because, despite the way I'd constantly misjudged you, you didn't detest me as much as I deserved.'

'Oh, Rico...' Tears flooded her eyes. 'I fell in love with you a long time ago, but I never realised it until I saw you again.' She saw joy illuminate his face and hurried on before he could speak, her voice trembling with misery, 'But you still don't understand!'

As briefly as she could she told him about David and Rosemary and their lovely child that she had brought up as her own.

He listened intently without interruption, waiting for her to finish before lacing his fingers through her dark hair and turning her face upwards to receive his kiss. For several seconds his mouth possessed hers with a proprietorial adoration that left her gasping.

'Do you think I should love Laurie any less because of this?' he asked tenderly. 'Is this why you hesitate to give me the answer I want?'

'No, it's not that,' she hastened to assure him, confident that he would have welcomed Laurie with the same open-hearted affection he bestowed on his brother's children. 'But I can't possibly marry you, Rico. I have to go on living in England. It's why I married David! Oh, don't you see!' She searched his still face with eyes luminous with tears as she rejected the promise of earthly paradise. 'David left me everything he owned on the understanding that it would be used for Laurie's future. It's a trust, a sacred duty, something I can never turn my back on. I have to raise her in England as David and

Rosemary would have done, provide the house and environment that's rightly hers. If I uproot her I'll have betrayed the two people who befriended me when I most needed it as well as a young child entrusted to my care!'

The ensuing silence was broken by a solitary cicada perched somewhere in the garden, before Rico spoke again.

'I can't leave Spain, Merle. My life, my future are here at the clinic. There's no way I could live in England.'

'I never expected you to.' She winced at the harshness of his tone. Not for a single moment had she considered he would make such a sacrifice. There would always be another woman available, and Rico de Montilla belonged to Spain, to the warmth and beauty of Andalusia and the eminent career he was carving out for himself. It was something she had always recognised and respected.

'But I can't let you disappear from my life!' He gathered her even closer, running his hands down her trembling back, finding her mouth again with his own, easing her away so that his seeking hand could find the swelling mound of her breast, closing his fingers over it as his kiss became deeper and more urgent.

For several seconds Merle savoured his embrace, enjoying the sensual responses of her own body. Then he was holding her away from him, staring down at her dazed face, her pleasure-swollen mouth, with haunted eyes.

'We'll see each other when I come here on holiday. We can still be friends.' Even as she said it she knew the futility of such a suggestion.

'Friends!' he grated. 'After what has just happened between us? Do you really imagine I could be in the same room, on the same beach, sitting at the same table, without wanting to take you to my bed and love you until you cried for mercy?'

She stared at him, blindingly aware that he spoke the truth, sharing his feelings.

'I tried to stop this happening,' she told him through parched lips. 'I wanted you to go on despising me so that the temptation never arose. That's why I didn't tell you I was a widow or that David and I had never been lovers. I wanted you to go on thinking I was meretricious and wanton...'

'Stop it, Merle!' His hand rose to silence her mouth with a velvet touch. 'I tried to believe those things because I was hurt and jealous, but it was impossible. The attraction between us was always more than physical, a mixture of chemistry and spirit. When you stood on my doorstep that first night I tried to persuade myself that I hated you, but I always knew it was a lie. If you were in trouble I had to help you, and heaven forgive me, I wanted to savour the pleasure of sharing my house with you even if it was for such a brief time. I thought you were forbidden fruit and I swore not to repeat Adam's sin a second time, but I could look, couldn't I—and fantasise a little without incurring damnation?'

'There'll be another girl in your life, someone who will love you as much as I do. A girl who shares your background and whom you find irresistible.' Merle tried to console him, although unreasonable jealousy tortured her at the very idea.

'Not second best—I'll never settle for that. If I can't have you, then I shall never marry!' The white torment on his face shocked her to the core of her being, but she could only shake her head, denying him hope.

'Then there's nothing more to be said. We have reached a *callejón sin salida*—a road with no exit, no?'

'Yes.' It was as much as Merle could do to speak as her throat muscles knotted in a lump large enough to choke her.

'Then we may as well be leaving.'

Rico didn't wait for her answer but turned on his heel and made for the door. Merle lingered in the sunny kitchen for a few more seconds, fighting and winning the battle to avoid breaking down completely. That would come later when she was in the privacy of her own room. Having Rico detest her had been pain enough. Having him love her was an agony against which she needed every shred of her courage if she were to survive the coming days.

'When am I going to meet this mysterious benefactor I've heard so much about?' Barbara twisted in front of the long mirror, admiring herself in a black off-the-shoulder blouse and long floral cotton skirt.

'Rico?' Merle looked up from filing her nails, casting an approving glance at her sister. 'You look gorgeous in that, Barbie.'

'Of course Rico.' Barbara refused to be side-tracked. 'I must have met the entire Montilla clan this afternoon, with the exception of the guy who rescued our holiday home.'

'It *was* rather like Victoria Station, wasn't it?' Merle remembered, her eyes lighting with laughter. 'As a matter of fact, Armando, Ramón and his family had only just arrived back after a tour of the *cortijo* when Enrico delivered you from the airport.'

'Do you know, that's the first time I've seen you laugh since I arrived?' The older girl studied her sister reflectively. 'I thought you looked a bit strained when I first saw you, but I wasn't going to say anything in front of

Grant and the children, but now we're alone I hope you're going to confide in me.'

'There's nothing to confide.' Merle smoothed the last nail, before discarding the file and rising to her feet. For a zombie she was coping extraordinarily well with events, she flattered herself. 'Come on, it's time we went and joined the party. We've been talking so much I didn't realise how late it was getting. Pavane will think we've deserted her.'

'No, not yet, love.' Barbara spun round from the mirror, barring her exit. 'We may have been talking all afternoon, but not about anything meaningful. Something's upset you—and you still haven't told me when I'm going to meet this Rico. I've got a feeling the two things may be connected!'

Merle hesitated for a moment, faced with her sister's concerned expression—and was lost. Too many times Barbara had been her friend and protector, her confidante.

'Oh, Barbie, it's awful! I love him so much, and it's hopeless!' She bit her lip, determined not to give way to the threatening tears that she felt gathering. She had drained herself dry during the hours of darkness, surely? Tonight was a celebration, not a wake, and she was determined to join in the fun.

Her sister's face became serious. 'You mean he's married?'

'No—oh, no. In fact he asked me to be his wife, but of course it's impossible.'

'Impossible—why?' Barbara's brow wrinkled in puzzlement. 'If you love each other...'

'How can you ask?' Astonished at her sister's re-action, Merle regarded her with amazed eyes. 'It's Laurie.'

'You mean he doesn't want her?' Barbara's soft eyes filled with compassion.

'It's not that.' Eagerly Merle denied her sister's suspicions. 'But you more than anyone know the promises I made to David. Rico's working as an orthopaedic surgeon in Cadiz. His life is here, and I, of course, have to stay in England with Laurie. You know the only reason David and I married was to ensure that she wouldn't have to go into a foster-home, that she'd continue to live in the house where she was born...' Despite her resolution Merle's voice broke. 'Please, Barbie, I don't want to discuss it. I'll get over it in time, you'll see.' She made a determined effort to reach the door. 'Listen, I can hear music outside on the terrace, and I'm dying to have a dance with Grant...'

'You're wrong, Merle!' To her dismay Barbara refused to move. 'You have to listen to me. You're too near to the problem to be seeing it clearly. Yes, sure, David married you for Laurie's sake, we all know that. But it had nothing to do with the house.'

'Barbie—please...' Near to breaking-point, Merle tried to prevent the older girl from continuing, gasping when, instead of allowing her to pass, Barbie took her by the shoulders and shook her gently.

'Merle, you little fool! If all David had wanted was to ensure that Laurie had the house and was financially well provided for, he could have appointed trustees, instructed a solicitor. When he married you he was getting for her the one thing he couldn't arrange legally. He was ensuring that she would be loved and cared for by someone who loved her as much as he did, as Rosemary did! If Rico loves you and wants to care for both you and Laurie, then does it really matter where it happens?'

'But the house...?' A wild tumultuous joy was building inside Merle as she stared into her sister's face.

Barbara had never lied to her or tried to protect her from reality. Was it really possible that she could bring Laurie here and not betray David's trust? Her sister's strong assertion had had the ring of truth to it, and Barbara had been a constant and sympathetic audience at the domestic drama in which she, Merle, had starred.

'Rent it out,' Barbie answered her question succinctly. 'Bank the money for her. Let her inherit it when she's old enough to decide whether she wants to live there or not. It's a beautiful house, I agree, but it's only bricks and mortar. If that's the only reason you've turned Rico down, you're not thinking straight!'

'If I dared believe it...' Her heart beating faster as a seed of hope began to grow, Merle clutched at Barbara's arm. 'I've never thought of it like that before.' Had she really been blind to David's real intentions? She pushed her dark hair away from her brow as if it would clear the mist from her mind.

'If you're convinced of this man's love for you and his willingness to take Laurie into his heart and home— then believe it,' Barbara encouraged softly. 'David would have wanted both of you to be happy. You can't be in any doubt about that.'

'I don't know...' But the pall of misery which had dampened her spirits was lifting. Barbie was right, she had been too close to the problem to see it clearly. Suddenly hope was streaming through her, bringing in its wake a golden stream of happiness, but she mustn't make any rash decisions. 'I'll have to think about it.'

'Then don't take too long,' Barbara hugged her, touching cheeks with her in a sisterly embrace. 'I haven't met your Rico yet, but if he's anything like his brothers I can't wait to welcome him to the family!' She grinned conspiratorially. 'You look beautiful, Merle.' Her soft eyes assessed the floating georgette. 'That's the prettiest dress you've ever had, and, now the smile's come back to your face, I don't think I've ever seen you looking lovelier. Heaven knows, if anyone deserves to find true happiness, it's you! The moon's bright, the music's sweet and everyone's celebrating—I may be a romantic, but it seems a perfect night to rethink your decision and put your young man out of his misery.'

The party was in full swing as Merle stepped out on to the terrace. Unable to resist taking another peep at Laurie in the nursery, she had let Barbie go downstairs by herself, confident Grant would be impatiently awaiting her appearance.

Looking at the sleeping child, her dark curls splayed on the pillow, she had tossed over in her mind her sister's advice, for the first time allowing herself to recollect the way David had broached the subject of marriage when he had received his negative prognosis.

As if a veil had been torn from her eyes, the more she thought about it the more she became convinced Barbara was indeed right. It hadn't been only material goods Laurie's father had wanted to preserve for his daughter, it had been *her* love—and that would never alter wherever she was or with whomever she shared her life!

Now, her eyes sparkling with new-found elation, she searched the terrace for Rico. He had disappeared from the *cortijo* before she had dragged herself down to breakfast that morning, but he had promised Pavane to be at the party—and, knowing Rico, she was sure he wouldn't break his word.

Anxiously she smoothed down her dress, her fingers shaking with anticipation. Suppose he had changed his mind about wanting to marry her? Suppose the proposal of marriage had been made in the heat of the moment? A cold shiver trickled down her spine.

'Señora Costain...' A deep voice behind her had her spinning round to meet the friendly smile of Fidelio Diaz. 'Doña Pavane tells me you wished to speak to me?'

'Ah, Señor Diaz.' Forcing a smile on her face, Merle held out her hand, wishing the meeting could have been postponed. Suppose Rico simply put in a courtesy visit and disappeared again before she could speak to him? 'I just wanted to thank you for acting on my behalf with Señor Sanchez. You did a marvellous job.'

'You flatter me, *señora*. All I did was to locate the man. If it hadn't been for Don Rico nothing could have changed his mind.' He sighed as Merle looked bewildered. 'He is not an avaricious man, you understand. He had long since decided not to pursue the debt, but when he learned the extent of his granddaughter's disablement and the cost of the only operations which could help her, he realised he had the means of paying for them by taking the matter to court.'

'I'm not sure I understand,' Merle searched the lawyer's face for enlightenment. 'What operations?'

Fidelio Diaz looked surprised. 'Perhaps I do not explain myself so well in English. Sanchez's granddaughter was born with a badly deformed leg. The doctors suggested amputation, but there was an alternative, a series of bone implants over a number of years, but the cost would run into many millions of pesetas, so when Don Rico offered his professional services free plus accommodation at the clinic in Cadiz Sanchez agreed to release the deeds to him, taking in full settlement only the original debt and the accrued interest.' He paused to study Merle's shocked face. 'But surely you knew this, *señora*?'

'No—no, I didn't.' Rico had made this fantastic gesture for her? Her heart seemed to somersault at the sheer enormity of his sacrifice.

'Perhaps I shouldn't have mentioned it...?' The lawyer appeared discomfited. 'I wouldn't want to be considered indiscreet.'

'No, I'm glad you did. What you've just told me confirms a decision I made a few minutes ago.' Merle flashed him a dazzling smile. 'Now if you'll forgive me, I have to find someone...'

Just when disappointment was a hard knot in her chest and she was about to return to the *sala* to question Pavane about Rico's intentions, Merle saw his tall figure standing alone in the shadows, apart from the crowd, beneath the cluster of the lemon trees that edged the patio.

From a distance of a few yards their eyes met, his darkly courteous, hers sparkling with anticipation mixed with apprehension. Her heart was thumping like that of a trapped animal as she weaved her way through the dancing couples towards him. How magnificent he looked, wearing a light jacket over dark trousers, his face starkly handsome in the filtered light of the decorative lanterns.

'Merle...' He acknowledged her presence with a slight bow of his head as if she were a stranger, and she couldn't help but notice the lines of pain etched round his beautifully sensuous mouth as he let his eyes travel over her with a restrained yet hungry appreciation. 'You look more beautiful every time I see you.'

'Thank you,' she said breathlessly, her eyes glowing with the love it was impossible to hide. 'Rico, I've just spoken to Señor Diaz. He told me about Sanchez's granddaughter—how you purchased Paraiso with your time and your skill.'

'He should have been more discreet.' Anger tightened his jaw. 'The matter is entirely between Sanchez and myself.' He paused, his dark gaze travelling over her face as if he would imprint it on his memory for ever. 'However, since you've discovered it, you'll understand why it was impossible for me to consider living in England. The surgery is complicated and protracted. The child will need careful monitoring every month over a period of at least five years.'

'You mean—if it hadn't been for your promise you would actually have considered giving up your home and your job to start afresh in England?' Merle stared at him aghast. In her wildest dreams she had never thought to ask for so great a renunciation.

'Why not?' he asked tightly. 'If, unlike you, I hadn't been bound by a moral tie I wouldn't have let any frontier stand between us. Ironical, isn't it?' He smiled without amusement. 'I was determined to get Paraiso back for you, yet its attainment devastated all my dreams. It was to have been my wedding gift to you—as it is, I must ask you to accept it as a farewell present.'

'No, that's impossible.' Firmly she shook her head, adding before he could remonstrate, 'You see, I'm not going anywhere...but I will accept it as a wedding present.' She smiled up into his startled face, seeing a dawning hope bring fire to his sombre eyes. 'That is—unless you've changed your mind.'

'What are you saying, Merle?' Rico reached out his hands and she slid between them, nestling up against his tautly held body, alerted by the hoarseness of his voice to the extent of his reaction.

'That Barbara's made me see things in a different light. I've thought things over and I realise that David would never have entrusted Laurie to me unless he'd had absolute faith in my judgement,' she confessed simply. 'He knew I'd never contemplate marriage unless I believed my future husband would treat her as his own child.

Barbie made me see that it's not where we live that matters but with whom...'

She would have said more, gone on to explain that since speaking to Barbara she had decided to offer the rental of the house to her sister and Grant, for who else would make better custodians of Laurie's property? But Rico stopped her mouth by the most effectual means possible, his lips warm and erotically persuasive as they moved on hers, causing a sigh of pleasure to shudder through her.

She was trembling as he released her, her senses filled with the taste and touch of him, the erotic scents of fresh linen, subtle cologne and the indefinable essence that was Rico himself. She shuddered in delight as he buried his mouth in the perfumed skin at the curve of her neck and shoulder, moving it downward to discover the tender swell of her breast within the soft georgette neckline of her dress. She gasped with delight, and her hands rose to hold his head, her fingers tangling in the dark softness of his hair, her body aflame with desire.

'I thought I should never hold you again, never kiss you...' he whispered huskily. 'The hours since we've been apart have been a torment I wouldn't wish my worst enemy to share. I couldn't let you go, yet because I loved you I dared not try to force you against your own judgement, in case you grew to hate me.'

'I could never hate you.' Merle strained against the eager strength of his body, delighting in the knowledge that he was aroused by her softness and the perfume of her hair and skin.

'*Por Dios*, Merlita...!' His breath rasped as he pulled away from her to gaze into her expressive face. 'If we stay here we shall become a spectacle to rival the flamenco dancers whose performance begins soon. We should tell Armando, I think, that there is yet one more

event to celebrate tonight and that he'd better prepare
the family chapel for a wedding.'

'But not too soon...' Merle's blue eyes pleaded for
his understanding. 'Not before Laurie's got to know
you—and like you.'

'You mean to make me wait a week?' Laughter lent
a boyish charm to his splendid features. 'Agreed, *mi
corazón*, on one condition—you allow me my own
private celebration before we break the news to our
family and friends.'

'You mean now?' she asked tremulously, knowing
perfectly well that he did.

He didn't disappoint her, letting his eyes roam over
her parted lips, the classic line of her throat and
shoulders, his eyes flaring with passion beneath his
lowered lashes, 'I mean now, *mi corazón*,' he agreed
softly, 'and afterwards we shall seek out Esteban, who
has been demanding quite imperiously that I shall
summon you forth to be introduced to Isadora.'

'She's here with him?' Delightedly Merle saw his nod
of assent. 'That evening when you saw him holding my
hands...'

'Yes, I know,' he smiled shamefacedly. 'He told me
when I drove him back to the hacienda.'

'And you still came to my room!' If she had been less
happy her indignation would have been greater.

'I needed an excuse to see you, *amada mia*, and I was
mad with frustration and self-doubt. Even if you didn't
want him—you'd made it clear you didn't want me either
unless I gave you something more valuable than myself
alone, and that was a hurt that still smarted!'

'It wasn't true,' pleaded Merle, searching his
expression with troubled eyes. 'I only said it because I
thought to admit that I wanted you too would only lower
me further in your estimation—if that were possible.'

'And that was never true either, *dulzura mia.*' The power of his gaze transfixed her as he swallowed with effort. 'Sometimes pride acts like a poison which corrupts the mind, but love proved a powerful antidote. Prove to me that you are as compassionate as you are desirable and tell me you forgive me.'

'Perhaps...' But her smile told him what her lips withheld, as the tension left his shoulders. 'When you've made a perfect apology.'

In the soft dimness of her bedroom Rico smoothed away the flimsy georgette from her unresisting body until it lay in a crumpled heap on the floor, before lifting her and carrying her towards the bed. As she relaxed on its softness Merle watched him discard his own clothing with a joyous anticipation of the pleasures ahead.

There was no doubt left in her mind now but that she had made the right decision. She thought briefly of Barbie and Grant enjoying the house in England for a token rent until they had saved enough money to buy their own property; of the possibility of persuading her mother to come to Spain for her wedding; of Laurie having new cousins to play with and perhaps, in time, a brother or sister—then Rico joined her, drawing her into his arms, and she held him closely, her fingers playing lightly on his back as she recalled that moment long ago when she had first felt the unwitting pangs of love for him, and after that there was no thought of anything but the splendour of the moment and the fulfilment of her dreams.

HARLEQUIN
Romance®

**This September, travel to England
with Harlequin Romance
FIRST CLASS title #3149,
ROSES HAVE THORNS
by Betty Neels**

It was Radolf Nauta's fault that Sarah lost her job at the hospital and was forced to look elsewhere for a living. So she wasn't particulary pleased to meet him again in a totally different environment. Not that he seemed disposed to be gracious to her: arrogant, opinionated and entirely too sure of himself, Radolf was just the sort of man Sarah disliked most. And yet, the more she saw of him, the more she found herself wondering what he really thought about her—which was stupid, because he was the last man on earth she could ever love....

Harlequin Superromance®

**Available in Superromance this month
#462—STARLIT PROMISE**

STARLIT PROMISE is a deeply moving story of a
woman coming to terms with her grief and gradually
opening her heart to life and love.

Author Petra Holland sets the scene beautifully, never
allowing her heroine to become mired in self-pity. It
is a story that will touch your heart and leave you
celebrating the strength of the human spirit.

**Available wherever Harlequin books
are sold.**

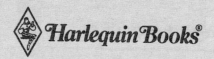 **Harlequin Books®**

GREAT NEWS...

HARLEQUIN UNVEILS NEW SHIPPING PLANS

For the convenience of customers, Harlequin has announced that Harlequin romances will now be available in stores at these convenient times each month*:

Harlequin Presents, American Romance, Historical, Intrigue:

> May titles: April 10
> June titles: May 8
> July titles: June 5
> August titles: July 10

Harlequin Romance, Superromance, Temptation, Regency Romance:

> May titles: April 24
> June titles: May 22
> July titles: June 19
> August titles: July 24

We hope this new schedule is convenient for you.

With only two trips each month to your local bookseller, you'll never miss any of your favorite authors!

*Please note: There may be slight variations in on-sale dates in your area due to differences in shipping and handling.

*Applicable to U.S. only

HDATES-RR

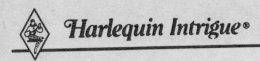
Harlequin Intrigue®

Trust No One . . .

When you are outwitting a cunning killer, confronting dark secrets or unmasking a devious imposter, it's hard to know whom to trust. Strong arms reach out to embrace you—but are they a safe harbor . . . or a tiger's den?

When you're on the run, do you dare to fall in love?

For heart-stopping suspense and heart-stirring romance, read Harlequin Intrigue. Two new titles each month.

HARLEQUIN INTRIGUE—where you can expect the unexpected.

Have You Ever Wondered If You Could Write A Harlequin Novel?

Here's great news—Harlequin is offering a series of cassette tapes to help you do just that. Written by Harlequin editors, these tapes give practical advice on how to make your characters—and your story—come alive. There's a tape for each contemporary romance series Harlequin publishes.

Mail order only

All sales final

Clip this coupon and return to:

HARLEQUIN READER SERVICE
Audiocassette Tape Offer
3010 Walden Ave.
P.O. Box 1396
Buffalo, NY 14269-1396

I enclose my check/money order payable to HARLEQUIN READER SERVICE for $5.70 ($4.95 + 75¢ for delivery) for EACH tape ordered. My total check is for $ _____
Please send me:

☐ Romance and Presents   ☐ Intrigue
☐ American Romance   ☐ Temptation
☐ Superromance   ☐ All five tapes ($21.95 total)

Name: _____

Address: _____ Apt: _____

City: _____ State: _____ Zip: _____

NY residents add appropriate sales tax.   AUDIO-H1D

HARLEQUIN
American Romance®

From the Alaskan wilderness to sultry New Orleans...from New England seashores to the rugged Rockies...American Romance brings you the best of America. And with each trip, you'll find the best in romance.

Each month, American Romance brings you the magic of falling in love with that special American man. Whether an untamed cowboy or a polished executive, he has that sensuality, that special spark sure to capture your heart.

For stories of today, with women just like you and the men they dream about, read American Romance. Four new titles each month.

HARLEQUIN AMERICAN ROMANCE—*the love stories you can believe in.*

AMERICAN